A Portent of Fallen Stars

Chronicles of the Grigori

Book 3

A Third Heaven Novel

by

Donovan M. Neal

© 2021 Donovan M. Neal

All rights reserved. No part of this publication may be reproduced, distributed, or transmitted in any form or by any means, including photocopying, recording, or other electronic or mechanical methods, without the prior written permission of the publisher, except in the case of brief quotations embodied in critical reviews and certain other noncommercial uses permitted by copyright law.

For permission requests, write to the publisher, addressed "Attention: Permissions Coordinator," at the email below:

tornveil@donovanmneal.com

Scriptures marked KJV are taken from the King James Version of the Bible (KJV): King James Version, public domain

Printed in the United States of America
ISBN: 9798755797085

Dedication

I dedicate this book to those who dare to dream and see it through to completion. May your imagination ever lead you to new realms.

Forward

To everything there is a season. In this last book of the Chronicles of the Grigori I pen what I expect to be my final dabblings into the world of the Third Heaven. If you are reading these words you have trully been a fan and have followed this journey as I explored the fall of Lucifer, the Old Testament, the birth of Christ, his ministry and victory over death Hell and the grave, his triumpant return.
By reading this series the Chronicles of the Grigori you have let me know that you wanted more. You like me have learned to love these characters, this world and the biblical truths these stories have communciated.

Yer here we are at the final book of the seond series in the Third Heaven universer, and my emotions are mixed. There is a sense of relief, but also slight sadness.

You've endured my birth into wrtiing marketable fiction with a speculative Christian bent. You've seen my mistakes, my growth and yet you are still here.

I can never thank you enough for encouraging me. Because of you I will continue to write stories that I hope both move and entertain.

With that promise I relase this final book into the earth and ask that you follow into me new storeis.

With love in Christ,

Donovan Neal

Table of Contents

Act I

Prime Realm: The Future..................................P.2

Act II

Chi Realm: The Ancient Past..........................P.88

Act III

The Journey of Henel James..........................P. 163

Glossary P.230

The Great Angelic Houses of Heaven P.242

Articles of War..P.249

Thank You...P.251

About the Author...P.252

Acknowledgments

To the Lord Jesus Christ, who loves me.

To my children Candace, Christopher and Alexander–you can do great things!

To the authors, comic book artists and writers who have come before, and who unknowingly have breathed on the embers of my imagination.

To all my beta readers and friends who shared both critiques and encouragement.

To my wife Nettie, who cheered me on when I had nothing and said, "Wow!" after reading the prologue of my first novel.

May God truly bless you all.

Scriptures

Genesis 50:20 But as for you, ye thought evil against me; *but* God meant it unto good, to bring to pass, as *it is* this day, to save much people alive.

Romans 9:19 Thou wilt say then unto me, Why doth he yet find fault? For who hath resisted his will?

Romans 8:29 For whom he did foreknow, he also did predestinate *to be* conformed to the image of his Son, that he might be the firstborn among many brethren.

Romans 8:30 Moreover whom he did predestinate, them he also called: and whom he called, them he also justified: and whom he justified, them he also glorified.

Jas 4:13-15
Come now, you who say, "Today or tomorrow we will go into such and such a town and spend a year there and trade and make a profit"— yet you do not know what tomorrow will bring. What is your life? For you are a mist that appears for a little time and then vanishes. Instead you ought to say, "If the Lord wills, we will live and do this or that."

"When you pray for Hitler and Stalin how do you actually teach yourself to make the prayer real? The two things that help me are (a) A continual grasp of the idea that one is only joining one's feeble little voice to the perpetual intercession of Christ who died for these very men. (b) A recollection, as firm as I can make it, of all one's own cruelty; which might have blossomed under different conditions into something terrible. You and I are not at bottom so different from these ghastly creatures." -- C.S. Lewis, Letters (1951)

Recap

Henel James, the reporter from the Jerusalem Post, has traveled from Earth of Heaven to meet with Argoth, head of the angelic order known as the Grigori. His questions have led the angel to reveal the actions that were precursory to the fall of Lucifer. An event started with one angel by the name of Lilith, who not content to abide in his calling, starts a chain reaction of events cascading and rippling reality. Yet Argoth's tale is not just what preceded mankind, but the angel explains another purpose behind Henel's visit to Heaven. Yeshua has a mission for the journalist. A mission that will help the remaining family member in Henel's life: his father: a mission into the ancient realm of Limbo.

Act I

Prime Realm: The Future

Argoth walked Henel into the basement of Heaven. It was a dimly lit room with blue lanterns that illuminated the stairwell. The temperature cooled as the two descended, and though the light of God penetrated all things in Heaven, there was something about the space that seemed to consume the light; something about the place hungered.

Henel found the hair on his arms standing on end and he started shivering and his breath became visible.

Argoth noticed his discomfort and spoke to the man. "Be not afraid. You are descending towards an entrance to Limbo, Henel James. And as we descend, you will notice that the warmth of El's presence seeps away from this place. For the felt presence of God is always warmest where his will is inviolate. But Limbo is the place where his will is allowed to be contested. And as we move deeper; know that you will experience… discomfort."

Henel replied, "How is that possible here in Heaven?"

"Because El hath not yet made a new Heaven and a new Earth. And upon that day, there will be no place where sin may exist to dampen the warmth and life that emanates from El. Until that day, his will may be defied. Creation hast not experienced the solidification of volition that our kind now possess, for those of my kind that would fall have fallen, and those of us who remain faithful to God cannot be moved from our state of allegiance. However, there is yet one more test to your kind to see who is worthy to see the next universe."

Henel was taken aback and replied, "Wait, you mean after the thousand years of Yeshua's reign there is still more trying of humanity that must come?"

"I have said, all I can say, but it is clear you have not studied the scrolls that El has left your people."

Henel ruminated on what Argoth meant and determined to learn more after he completed his mission. Yeshua had sent Henel to deliver the gospel to his father, who was in a coma, but how he was to reach him in a comatose state was beyond him. But he had seen enough that he knew Yeshua could do anything. And if God said Henel would relay the call of Christ to his father, whom he had not seen in twenty-five years; it could be done.

Further, the two walked down a winding staircase until they emerged into a massive room bathed in blue light. The walls and floors were carved with angelic runes. "The handwriting of God?" Henel asked.

Argoth nodded and replied. "The handwriting of God."

Each rune glowed and blue light pulsated over the walls and moved like the heated air in the desert, playing tricks with one's eyes.

The floor was a mix of dirt and stone. And Argoth continued his determined trek into the room.

Twenty-four giant pillars with glyphs written on them held up the palace. As Henel walked past several pillars, he recognized one symbol from his studies of ancient Hebrew. "Is this the symbol for Alpha?"

Argoth nodded in the affirmative as he watched the human examine the pillars and motioned Henel to the bright light that unleashed waves of fluorescent cobalt colors that bathed the room in sapphire.

A pulsating hum echoed throughout the chamber and Argoth walked to the edge of the light and Henel noted that a door could be seen beyond the light. A beckoning gate that was awash in blue.

"Behold Henel, son of James. The Gate of Limbo. Beyond this door lies the alternate possibilities of creation's path. Some to good and others to evil. Beyond this door Janus hath prepared a path that you may travel safely to accomplish the will of Yeshua. Do not deviate from this path. Lest you be lost to the eddies of temporal currents. Now see to your father. Learn what you must and be about the Lord's business."

Henel stood before the giant gate. It towered over him as he approached it. A door meant for something much larger than him, much larger even than angels. Henel swallowed hard and turned from the gate and queried Argoth.

"How will I return? And what if I fail?"

Argoth smiled, "Go Adamson, walk by faith and not by sight. God has chosen you to do this task, and there is no failure in God. Be not afraid. I have requested that Janus watch thee from afar and to act as thy guide you might find your way home."

Henel sighed in resolution that to ask further questions would be pointless. He did not leave Earth and parlayed with the head of the Grigori to be denied his answers. He would face this door: this causeway of what could be and what both was and is. And he would venture to see what the end would be.

Henel raised his head and covered his eyes to help shield against the blinding light and proceeded to enter what angels had named the Realm of Choices.

The Prime Realm: The Distant Past

All Grigori have a sacred duty to record the happenings of creation. A duty assigned to the race of ethereal angels by God himself. Lotan, the first of all Grigori, was given charge to oversee the realm of Limbo: the wilderness of discarded choices and a realm of alternative possibilities. Lotan prior to his departure separated the house of Grigori into three clans. The clan of the Archivist who are responsible for documenting the past. The clan of Parelthon: The Watchers: the recorders of the events of all things present. And finally, the Order of Mellontikos: those Grigori who are given the God-sight and are able to see into the future. They record the secret things of God and preserve the promises of God towards Creation. The Sephiroth was the title of the Head of House Grigori: The greatest among the Grigori clans who was able to walk in past, present and future. Lotan was first to possess this title, and it was he who understood the Lord's plan among all three phases of time. Thus, the Grigori were a race of angels whose function was to serve as the historians of Creation. A task told by Lotan from God to his people. For El had shared with Lotan a vision: a vision he was faithful to impart to all with the God-sight; that the dead, small and great, would one day stand before God; and all the books the Grigori had compiled would be opened: and a particular book was opened, which was the book of life: and the dead were judged out of those things which were written in the books, according to all their works. And Lotan then set three according to their clans and instructed them to teach all things that El had given and that if needed he would be seated upon a Tempest Throne to prevent the convergence of realms from colliding. And to sanctify Heaven from the Mists that El had shown would arise from his choice to give free will to four races within Creation. And the three created to bring the order of House Grigori to pass were Raphael, Janus, and Argoth. For it was Lotan who first walked with Lucifer invisibly when he and El first entered the Kiln.

* * *

Batriel Grigori of the order of Paron ruminated on the origins of his house and wondered how helping his charge Jerahmeel would cause Creation to arrive at the point where the books of house Grigori could be opened and all those living and dead would be judged. A day he and all his kind looked forward to. For upon that day House Grigori would be released to document no longer. A day of promise when Grigoric pens could be laid down and styli no longer must record the tales of others. Then the Grigori would be discharged to discover a new creation and a new Earth and to explore a new level of journaling to showcase the wonders of God: a mission different from that given to his kind now. A mission he looked forward to pursuing one day.

Batriel hovered past more of his kind. Each Grigori looked at him curiously as he floated without Jerahmeel. And wherever Batriel went, the Grigori that saw him resisted the urge to explore this wonder of a Grigori with no charge. He watched as his kind turned their heads and stared at him as he finally arrived at the door of a large conference room. The room was the meeting room of Michael Kortai, Lord of House Kortai, and one of the seven spirits that stood before the Lord God Almighty.

He entered the room where Michael was standing reviewing maps and documents while several members of his House discussed building plans. He then did a thing which few of his kind have ever done. He materialized to be seen.

"Ahem," said Batriel. "My apologies Lord Michael, but I require a word and it is urgent."

All the angels looked up and immediately looks of confusion and concern washed over the group. "Is this a Grigori?" said one.

Michael then replied, "Leave us."

Michael's comrades looked at their leader and bowed as each slowly wrapped up their maps they walked themselves past the Grigori, staring and exited the room. Batriel closed the door behind them, and Michael spoke.

"For what reason does a Grigori appear to me, for surely a

Watcher has a charge?"

Batriel bowed, "Indeed, the thing is as you say, my Lord. And I come at the exhortation of my charge. Lord Jerahmeel is in extreme danger and demands that Heaven be prepped for assault."

Michael scrunched his eyes and shirked back, "Assault? What in Creation could assault Heaven and her Host?"

"Lord Jerahmeel now stands in the basement of Heaven and is all that lies between an incursion of Limbo and its entrance to Heaven. For Limbo is disquieted and the Mists now spill from her boundaries and seek escape into our realm: an escape that will lead them here. I now have come to give thee his words and to make known to thee the events recorded in the book of Jerahmeel."

"Show me." replied Michael.

Batriel then lifted his hand, and a book appeared and from the book an image filled the room and showed Jerahmeel and Batriel talking, and Michael listened to the conversation as recorded by Batriel.

"These creatures.... will they penetrate the shield?" said Jerahmeel.

"Yes," replied Batriel.

"What is the nature of the Mist, and can it harm us?"

"The Mists are the unselected choices of Creation seeking flesh. The refuse of decisions contrary to God... sin is the word El hath used to describe the manifestations, and these have been deposited in a realm shut off from angelic kind. They are a degenerative cloud that, if exposed to in long durations, will in time turn one away from his majesty and change the truth of God into a lie, and cause one to worship and serve the creature more than the Creator. These are the Mists, and they are locked away in the wilderness that is Limbo, and the land is governed by the first Grigori: Lotan the Tempest King."

"Is this who Raphael has gone to seek help?"

"I do not know this thing. But if the Mists have leeched from the portal into this realm, then something is amiss, for it is not the norm for the Withering to venture beyond Limbo's domain."

"The Withering…?"

"Aye, High Prince. It is the name given by the Grigori to the Mists. Their presence corrupts all things. However, to permit the possibility of love, El hast allowed for the expression of choices counter to his own. Limbo cannot hold the Mists for all time. Another feature must at some point address the variable that is love. But El hast yet to reveal this feature. We have evidence to believe that there is yet another domain that in time El will create that will subsume the realm of choices and will be the permanent solution to all sentience that would choose to live apart from Him."

Jerahmeel pondered the words given him and replied, "Can

you give a message to the Lord Michael and Gabriel?"

"We are not connected in that manner, my prince. Only one of us: the chief prince, can connect with all. I must leave my post to carry a message to the Grigori of the princes."

Jerahmeel nodded in understanding. "You deem your mission to chronicle me more important than all things? Know that I understand and respect your duty." Jerahmeel looked as the shield Raphael had erected slowly gave way against the now concerted onslaught of vaporous cloud-like creatures that pummeled the same point repeatedly.

"Query Grigori: how long do you project the boundary between the Mists and the Chief Prince of thy house to hold?"

The floating angel was silent for a moment and then replied, "At the rate upon which the creatures smite the shield wall, it will experience a total collapse in but a matter of hours."

"And what danger will Heaven be subject to?"

"The Mists will seek to feed upon the denizens of the land, their choices will be subsumed and eternity and yea, all of creation will be subject to the corruption that is Sin."

Jerahmeel then made himself perfectly clear. "WE will not let this be. YOU are hereby commanded to leave me and carry this message to Prince Michael and Gabriel. Let them know we are under attack and to muster all forces at the basement of heaven that we might stop the encroachment of the Mists. A pinch-point will they have there so that the numbers of the Mists that would swell through this gate will count for nothing. Let them know I will hold off the barrage and give Heaven as much time as possible to gather her strength. Relay Grigori the seriousness of what you see here today and relay that I stand alone as a standard between Limbo and the Capital. If need be, urge the Lumazi to summon the Ophanim and Seraph to uphold the treaty of the Parliament of Angels' call. For, though the Withering may start at the door of angels… it will surely not end there. Are you clear in your purpose, Grigori?"

Batriel was silent for a moment. He looked at the shield of the Lord of his house and then at Jerahmeel, who began to slowly amour himself to prepare for battle and then nodded in understanding.

"I will do as you say. May the Lord watch between me and thee, whilst we are absent one from another."

The image then faded into nothing and Batriel closed the book and it too disappeared into his purple robes.

"The word has been given to you, Prince Michael of House Kortai. Do not let it not return void."

Batriel then bowed and turned to exit, and Michael called out after him. "Grigori, where are you going?"

Batriel then spoke over his shoulder, "To return to my charge.

Whether he be dead or alive, I will be by his side to record every jot and tittle. I trust, high prince, that the Lord Gabriel will be given this message per the Harrada's request?"

Michael nodded. "When I am done, all of Heaven will have heard thy words. Return and know that soon the rest of Heaven will follow."

Batriel nodded and disappeared to return to Jerahmeel.

The Nexus: The Ancient Past

Michael of the Beta Realm and his men had tracked Lucifer through Limbo, confiscated his remaining accomplice, and had followed the temporal storm's origins to a shimmering hollow that seemed phased into the rock-walls that lined their sides.

Michael lifted his hand with a fist, and all those that followed him came to a halt.

"Azaniel, give me your sword." The angel did as bidden and forwarded his saber to the prince.

Michael took the blade and plunged it into the shimmering wall that pulsed with plasma. Its eeriness illuminated the pathway enough that travel forward could be seen.

Lilith replied, "We have reached the entrance to the Nexus. We must leave this channel before another storm is launched through this corridor."

Michael looked at the angel, nodded, then stepped forward into the dark plasma.

The sound of water emanated as he passed, and each member of the entourage followed their leader.

Michael stepped through the liquid like membrane of a door and entered a cavern. His eyes scanned the scene to see a great onyx throne that shimmered. Light pulsed intermittently from it and around it floated globules that crackled with shimmering lights that also crackled from within. Arcs of lightning leaped from one globule to another, and each tendril of energy ended at the base of the throne. It was then, as his eyes scanned the structure, that he saw the two beings that stood at the base of the steps of the throne.

Michael moved towards them as those that followed him made their way one by one through the watery-like membrane.

Immediately, the throne lit up as Michael drew near and bursts of plasma stretched out in screaming wails and then coalesced into a spherical ball of plasmic fury. The sound was as the howling of many winds and Michael and all present covered their eyes and attempted to find something to hold on to as the orbicular ball of energy launched and catapulted into the corridor even as several of Michael's men attempted to step through.

But they were too late, and those members of Michael's entourage that had not stepped through to safety screamed as their flesh was incinerated or their bodies were carried aloft by the temporal winds; winds that disassembled the constituent parts of all matter and then reassembled them again. Tearing at the microscopic fibers that atoms embraced. Each scream now floated upon the hurricane-like ailerons of tornadic winds. Bodies that lifted as flotsam and were now tossed about helplessly into the dark recesses of Limbo. And Michael and those that had survived looked on in horror as their comrades were no more.

Michael turned around in rage and eyed the chair before him and the two beings. One was a Grigori... the other... unknown.

But the chair was clearly the source of the storms that had plagued them. "This seat is a seat of power," said Michael. "And I claim it in the name of the Lord of Hosts. This is the seat of Limbo's rage, and I will claim this power, control it, and I will use it to destroy all of Heaven's enemies."

Lotan replied, "The Tempest Throne hast not been given to thee to administer. It is clear to me that you are awash in pride and act outside the station given thee. You have no power here to give... let alone to take."

Michael looked down at the two men who stood at the base but several yards from his position and replied. "Perhaps not, but nevertheless I will take it. Do you object?"

Lotan eyes narrowed, and arcs of electricity flickered from his hands to the entirety of his person and he replied. "I do. You do not know that there must always be one to sit upon the Tempest Throne. It is not a seat of power to yield, but a responsibility to wield. And you have not been appointed to be King of Limbo."

Michael then unsheathed his sword and several of his comrades formed three to his right and three to his left, and they too removed their swords from their scabbards.

Michael then smiled and sat in the chair, and his hand was atop the pummel of his sword. The throne immediately responded to his presence, and light emanated from the onyx chair. The ceiling and floor flickered as arcs and bolts of plasma suddenly stretched across the cavern. Raining bolts of lightning down upon the cavern. Raphael and Lotan watched as a sudden fog rolled across the cavern floor from beneath them, and whispers and forms coalesced and took shape.

Humanoid forms and monstrosities of smoke rose from the earthen floor.

Lotan looked at Raphael and spoke. "The angel cannot be allowed to remain on the throne or calamity will befall us all. If you wish to save your realm, yeah, Creation itself, then you will help me dislodge him. Even it means the dissolution of your kind."

Raphael thought about Lotan's words and understood the gravity of the situation. He had beheld a future where El had wiped out all of creation. And Raphael knew unless he joined Lotan in his endeavor to recapture the seat of Limbo. He was watching the beginning of the end of all things. For it was clear the Withering had descended upon Michael, and he had been in the realm too long. It was not Raphael's desire to kill his brother, nor any of his kind. But he sighed and resolved himself to do what must be done to secure Creation's survival.

Therefore, Raphael nodded in agreement, and his dagger materialized in the air near his head. He took a defensive stance and the two slowly made their way to ascend the stairs of the Tempest Throne to confront the alternative version of his realm's Prince of Kortai.

* * *

Raphael looked at Lotan, who advanced towards his throne. He followed the angel slowly, aware of what he was about to do, and then grabbed the true head of House Grigori by his shoulder.

"Hold on, great one. Perhaps reason can be the victor here and not force of arms."

Lotan looked at Raphael and then Michael, who sat upon the throne. He eyed the mists that were moving across the floor and opened his mouth to speak. "The Mists do not recognize this one here. The incense that now emanates from the throne is a strange fire to them. He must leave the seat of power, and if he will not leave, he must be dislodged. His presence upon its seat could target the capital itself with the power of temporal storms. Do what thou must. But do so quickly."

Raphael nodded, and he left Lotan to approach the base of the seat of Limbo. He sheathed his dagger and lifted his hands above his head.

Ares and those that surrounded Michael eyed the Grigori warily and spoke. "Lord Michael? Your orders, my prince?"

Waves of power emanated from the throne as he sat upon it. He felt the obsidian and traced his fingers against the ancient runes carved into the armrest of the chair. He looked at Raphael, who approached the throne's base and replied. "Hold your sword, Ares. Raphael of House Grigori, I know you. But I perceive you are not the Head of the House Grigori of my land. For my Raphael is dead. Who art thou and of more import… who is he that stands eying me and this place that we now dwell?"

The Nexus pulsated, and waves of sapphire energy shimmered on the walls and floor. And everywhere the eye beheld; ancient glyphs were etched into the walls and floor. And just past the point of the eyes, walls like water dripped from a source unknown and shimmering black globules hung suspended in the air.

Raphael looked back towards Lotan, who had not sheathed his weapons. He also looked at the swirling mists that increasingly churned over the ground.

"I am Raphael, head of house Grigori, Lumazi and thy brother. But it is as you say. I am not the Raphael that you know."

"And he…?" Michael pointed at Lotan.

"He," said Raphael. "Is a bit more complicated, but what I

can say is that he is the first Grigori: the keeper of the land that we both trespass and the King of Limbo. He is also losing patience with us. None of us can stay here. All of us are in danger. We have entered a domain that has been deemed off limits by El himself. The longer we persist, the more we stir forces we cannot control and yea even invite oblivion. You must surrender your position. Allow me to take Argoth here to his appointed place, and we all must leave."

Michael eyed the stirring of the fog that raced with increasing speed along the ground. "And this place… what is it?"

Raphael nodded, "I understand you seek understanding about the wonders and mystery of this place. But consider that El hast not made thee privy to that which he has placed behind the wall of his will. Who then am I to share what El hast not allowed by revelation?"

Michael considered the words spoken to him and replied. "Very well, but this one here." Michael pointed to Argoth, who stood shackled behind him. "This one here was in collusion with the Lucifer of my realm. His actions have contributed to the prevention of his apprehension. He is an accomplice to sedition. He will come with me."

Lotan then walked to where Raphael stood and raised his voice for all to hear. "Your presence here will not be tolerated. You will all leave… now."

The Chi Realm: The Ancient Past

Zadkiel loved God and the people of God.

Therefore, when the call came from the Chief Prince to assemble at the steps of the palace; Zadkiel held no hesitation. It was a call to glory, a call to follow those who had erred and strayed from the way; a call to restore a brother to the rightful order, for angels to be one. Therefore, the Host was assembled to compel an errant house; to show the degree that angels would follow to restore a brother into fellowship. A calculated move explained to show by example that the Host would cleave to its own.

Lucifer explained that House Grigori had seceded from the Parliament of Angels, an act that warranted a show of force and love to compel House Grigori to return. Zadkiel would therefore willingly display this love, and if necessary, employ the rod to compel obedience. For who could turn away from El and the Host? It was clear from Lucifer's explanations that Janus had possessed House Grigori. For even he had seen the phantom that appeared in the sky of Heaven; an image that beckoned the house to descend into the Gate of Limbo and to depart from this realm to a place off limits to angels.

Zadkiel was proud to follow Lucifer. Proud to be a part of the mission to escort Grigori home and save them from trespassing against God's will.

But that was then.

For now, all that stood before him was death.

Zadkiel had heard of a word called 'dissolution,' a term some angels had called the cessation of Elomic life. An angel that was created in the latter days of creation, Zadkiel now witnessed death firsthand, and it was nothing he had imagined.

For the angel had hidden himself in a cleft in a rock; hidden away from the Mists that flowed over the dank floor of the Realm of Choices. The same floor radiated the stench of dissolution: a stink akin to decayed fish. But death also had a color, and it was the gloom of grays and the dark shades of various blacks illuminated by hints of blue over the whole of the area.

Death also carried a sound: and it was of the screams and cries of mutilated friends that assaulted his ears; for no praise and worship pursed across the lips of his kind in this place. No exaltations of adoration rang in his ears. Nothing but the echoes of screams and pitiful cries of help draped in yelps of fear filled his hearing.

Yelps that moaned in a desperate choral harmony of blood gurgling death.

A sound that if he survived, was unlike the singing of sopranos, altos, and tenors that announced the arrival of El before his people.

No, the sounds that carried across this gloomy battle were the tenor and bass of angels who prayed to escape the cloud-like creatures that surrounded them all. Cumulus doppelgänger's that possessed mouths of fangs and tentacled tongues wrapped with incisors. Zadkiel watched creatures known as Zoa fall from the ceiling and shroud and consume angels alive while some lifted Harrada and Kortai off the ground as the creatures fought over angelic twisting bodies before they ripped them in their hunger-driven lust to devour angel flesh.

Angels fought with valor mixed with desperation, slicing at the dread fog with swords, mace and axes. But all sliced in vain as their weapons merely passed through living smoke. A smoke that entered the lungs of angels and that snatched the Breath of Life from them only to absorb the self-same life into the sentient clouds that were the Mists. An unstoppable fog that at will, would become tangible to accost the Host and destroy the legions that had dared to invade Limbo.

A massacre that Zadkiel watched in fear as he hid within the cleft of a rock.

Like all Grigori, his eyes recorded and burned into his memory what would be the decimation of the armies of Heaven; for phased Grigori fought with beings that also could become intangible at will. Grigoric daggers retracted then stabbed forward, but it was of no effect, for even the Grigori were also obliterated. As the Mists merely wrapped their ghostly forms into the phased forms of House Grigori and took the newfound bodies as their own.

Zadkiel watched as those he had come to compel with force, those he had hoped to return to the capital of Heaven; now fought with those that had come to hunt them. For the Host of heaven was arrayed as one against the Mists. An army united in their desire to survive in the basement of Heaven: a locale off limits to angelic-kind. A trespass the Host would now pay for with blood.

Zadkiel's eyes widened as he watched a rocky growth open its side to reveal a furnace of fire. Flames flickered from its makeshift mouth, and it bellowed out a mix of rage and anger stewed in an animalistic rumble akin to the great cats of Earth. A roar that shattered ancient columns before it, and from which even the Mists made room when it advanced in lava like increments.

From the cavern of the craggy beast's mouth belched worms; maggots of fire that inched across the floor of limbo as a tidal infestation of carrion upon those angels who had fallen. Each squirming larva entered or created orifices that burrowed into angelic flesh: maggots that moved as if controlled by a single consciousness. Slowly the creatures nestled within veins and muscle, quilting sinew to sinew and flesh to tendons. And Zadkiel heard a sound rattle through the deep places of Limbo, a sound of bones connecting to bones as angels that had fallen to the Mists or to one another now stood to their feet. An unholy army that walked in lumbering steps. An army hollowed of their own will and now animated by the will of another. And Zadkiel watched as the rising hill of rock and fire roared, and when it did, the animated corpses of angels marched forward and attacked members of the Host. Angel after angel fought to hold the now rising tide of celestial undead that advanced upon them. Zadkiel watched helplessly as the fiery maggots merely jumped from their hosts to the living. Angel after angel batted some larva away, only to be overtaken from the back, or the floor. Others merely turned to have a maggot jump into their open mouths, then expand over the face to devour the angel alive. Muffled screams and bodies rolled on the ground in vain attempts to withdraw the maggots from cheekbone and eyes, ear and throat. Muffled screams that inevitably would cease and leave a corpse pulsating on the ground with maggots that writhed within.

Corpses that burst open only to unleash even more of the devouring worms that animated the dead.

And though the Host seemed infinite; the dead were now a number that also melded into the whole. For Zadkiel, these were not just former combatants but angels who were friends, comrades… family. And now they stood but a wall of emaciated dripping flesh and hollowed eyes yearning to consume those they had afore entered the realm of Limbo in arms.

Zadkiel placed his hands over his ears for the screams of the dying and the grunts of those that fought to keep back the slow march of the living mountain was an ambient noise that now pervaded all things. For when Zadkiel turned to his left maggots controlled by the mountain of fire consumed all that they encountered, while to his right the Mists choked the life and or mirrored their attackers and drove their viewers mad for the images they showed to their flesh and blood counterparts. Images that showed their lusts amplified, images that caused the viewer to freeze in dismay, unable to move, frozen to see the display of sin that was possible for them to commit. An easy prey for the Mists to enter and snatch the life and leave but a warm carcass for the worms of living fire to consume.

A scene of death was all that the eyes of Zadkiel could see.

And Zadkiel too was frozen in place, unable to see that his hiding place was found and that the Mists beheld an angel hidden in a cleft with his hands over his ears. And his eyes were glazed and unblinking as the ghostly apparitions showed him images of despair, horror, and fear.

A cinematic diet he could not resist while fiery maggots inched their way towards him to consume him alive.

Worms that crawled over the now weeping eyes of the angel to enshroud him in eternal night.

Chi Realm: The Ancient Past

Janus was unconscious. His body strapped onto an onyx slab within the Halls of Annals.

Atop a podium was a vellum covered book that pulsated in light and was sealed with seven seals. The proverbial Book of Life: journal of the Almighty God. It was alleged that within the tome contained the animus of God. The unspent wrath of the Lord. Lilith beheld the book and noted that each seal was a different color and matched the colors of the rainbow. He reached out to touch one and something akin to a static shock leaped out at him.

"Arrgghh!" the angel cried. Immediately, he drew back his hand in pain. He cradled his hand and massaged it, for it had become numb and shook it repeatedly to restore its circulation.

The sharp pain was momentary but immeasurable to comprehend. His hand throbbed, and he contemplated his course of action to disclose the secrets of the Almighty. And as he did, Janice slowly awakened.

"Lilith… do not do this…"

Lilith looked down at his fellow Grigori and replied. "What would you have me do old friend? For I have seen my dissolution and have seen my death at the hands of him who I would call a friend. And perhaps if my death had been at the hands of an enemy… perhaps I could have borne it. But it was not from him that hated me, nor him that would magnify himself against me, that my death would ensue. For if so, perhaps I would have even hidden myself. But no, it was one of my own house, someone my equal, my guide in a darkness and an acquaintance. And did we not take sweet counsel together, and even walk into the house of God in company?"

Lilith harrumphed, "And yet you ask me to spare thee, when you know this future lies before me. A future that would see Raphael slay me in cold blood. And would thou have warned, nay moved to prevent my dissolution? Would you have spared me the actions I have taken to mark a different outcome? No, instead you also stand to oppose me. I have seen both you and Argoth travel over dimensions to apprehend me. How then should I react to bounty hunters who have been appointed by my future killer? What in the laws of God prohibits me from self-preservation?"

Janus sighed, "I have not seen the vision you purport. But yea, I have come at the command of the High Prince. And now have been forced to assume even the mantle of Sephiroth. But know Lilith. This also was a vision I did not see. Release me I pray you and we can discover together the option that would prevent this thing you fear. But to delve into the Book of Life is not the way. I beg of you, my friend. Do not do this thing. I am only beginning to understand what lies within, and what I have come to understand… to know is that the contents are neither meant for this time nor this place. Please Lilith, do not do this thing."

Lilith paused at the words of Janus. His eyes welled and his lip quivered as if he battled some great war within. His face then turned downward, and his brow furrowed and he replied.

"No. I will not accept my fate as seen. Nor will I be party to my own destruction. I have seen what is coming. A portent of falling stars. Angels who will be cast adrift along the meridian of the universe for opposing to bow the knee to God. And their crime? To have volition apart from his. I have seen Lucifer raise the Host in rebellion against El, who would consign those he deems disloyal into a living mountain of fire. A fire that would consume Elohim alive for a thousand years or more. I will not serve such a ruler. Nor give heed to the lackeys that do. I am sorry, but you have not seen what I have seen. Witnessed what I have beheld. There must be some way to stop what is coming. And if I must rip open the diary of God to divine those mysteries than your tome will be breached."

Lilith then frowned and his stylus appeared, and it changed into a dagger. He eyed the blade, then lowered his head.

"Lilith, don't do this." Janus pleaded.

Lilith raised his eyes, and they locked with those of Janus, and he walked towards the onyx slab towards which his Grigori brother lay and replied. "I am sorry."

He reached for Janus's strapped body and Janus attempted to mist and release himself. "It is of no avail, brother. The bindings can hold even thee." He then held his knife in the air over Janus' sternum and spoke. "Cor-see-afu" which in the Elomic tongue means 'to see.'

Seven seals of color then shown over Janus' naked flesh. Each seal was embedded within his skin. Janus, knowing Lilith's intent, shifted on the table; watching as Lilith lowered the blade towards the first seal that was embedded within his flesh.

"Lilith…" Janus pleaded.

"Lilith!!"

And Lilith, the housemate of Janus, brought his blade to his comrade's skin and began the slow and painful process of carving the seal from his friend's chest.

Janus then released screams into their sealed room. His supplications to cease falling on deaf ears as his body spasmed from the torturous agony until the angel fell into shock and his cries were silent.

The Prime Realm: The Ancient Past

There are tales that Jerahmeel, when vying to lead his house to show his wisdom, strength and mercy, froze his contenders in ice: each allegedly immobilized and helpless before him. It is said that he then eyed each of his three opponents to the point that they understood he could shatter them at his whim and send their entrails into oblivion. It was this display of power that was not just impressive, but what he did next that made all of House Harrada bow their knee as their angelic leader. It was the time he took to carefully chip away at the ice that he had encased them in and with a hammer and chisel; he removed each from their entrapment and took a towel and dried them until they were all made whole. When it was asked of him why he did not finish them? His response was recorded by the Grigori on this wise. "I am not here to destroy, but to serve my people. They cannot be served if they are dead. I will have mercy and not sacrifice."

But in the battle, to be the standard between the encroaching vapors that were the mists and to protect those who stood behind him, mercy and care were abandoned. For, with the frosted blade of his axe he swung it in the paths of the oncoming Mists. His blade chilled the air to sub-zero temperatures such that if a Zoa but passed through the zone, they froze in their tracks. Their statuesque bodies posed in positions of attack, only to be smashed into pieces by the hammer that swung in his opposing hand. A dance of destruction of shattered ice, and vapor crystallized. The bowels of the creatures lay before him as clumps of powdered snow.

With raised hands an orb of ice manifested in his open palm only to be thrown and let loose as an icy projectile into the throngs that approached him. Immediately upon contact with the ground a wall of ice sprung up before him, and as the vapors poured around to the left and to the right of a now existent barrier, his foes were hacked and hammered into dust. Jerahmeel's face was flushed as his eyebrows became filled with the snow like powder from his foes. His breath left his body in visible pants as he exerted himself. He did not have the power of Raphael to keep the horde of Limbo within the realm of choices. But he would be damned to see them pass to the upward places of the palace into Heaven.

"Back foul shades of gloom; for the light of Heaven's shore will not be darkened!"

Jerahmeel slammed the hilts of both his weapons into the now frozen floor and swells of ice launched as a tidal wave before him, freezing at least a dozen Zoa and spider-like creatures in ice. He then took his hammer and slammed the hilt into the ground and the wave of approaching frozen Zoa shattered into a million crystals of ice and the sound was as the collapsing of glaciers that plummet into the sea.

The detonating sound waves traveled upwards into the rooms, walls and columns that undergirded the palace and shook the floors and walls, causing dust to fall as snow from the ceilings.

Occupants of the palace stopped and considered what was the source of such movement, but it was Gabriel who, in a session with a steward of House Malakim, voiced the now apparent disturbance that was noticed by them all.

"What was that?"

Michael then burst into the room and the door slammed against the wall.

"Gabriel, we have a situation. Jerahmeel needs our help."

Gabriel extended his hand and his staff, which was leaning against a wall, moved of its own accord and rushed to his waiting palm.

"Where is Lucifer?" asked Gabriel.

"He is earth-side. Raphael is also on assignment. Assemble Sariel and Talus and meet me at the well of stairs."

Gabriel looked at him curiously. "The Basement of Heaven? Is there a problem within Limbo?"

Michael nodded. "I have been informed that the gate between dimensions is down and Jerahmeel abides alone. Now go and quickly find Talus and our brother that we might see ourselves if the things relayed to me are true."

Gabriel nodded and instantly became a blur, and his speed was such that he exited the door before Michael could close the entryway behind him, and each went their way to gather the strength of Heaven.

The Nexus: The Ancient Past

Argoth walked shackled behind Ares, who followed Michael and his cadre from the Beta Realm. They roamed the dimly lit earthen floors and ridges as they pressed their backs into a cliff as they made their way to what finally appeared to be the center of the Realm of Choices: The Nexus.

Shimmering water-like walls separated them from what seemed like a cavern within. Argoth strained his eyes to see what might be within the cavern. There was an energy field that emanated from the place and the air itself moved as if it was eager to be somewhere else.

"Michael, I would remind you that Lucifer only sought this place to escape from thy pursuit. Now that he is dead, is it wise to trespass the abode of the caretaker of this realm?"

Michael looked at his captive and replied, "For what purpose does the Grigori worry over the habitation of those, not Elohim?"

Argoth realized this Michael was harder than the prince he knew from his own realm and replied. "My anxiety would be over anything that might trifle with the word of God. And the word of God is known to all of our kind, yea and it is nigh thee, even upon your lips. This realm has been made off limits. Yet we persist in this domain as if the return of El's command will not bring recompense. I would hope that the High Prince would not be so cavalier towards God's command, that he must again be reminded of this fact; unless of course the High Prince now holds himself above the word of God itself?"

Michael stopped and looked at Argoth. He cracked a smile and spoke. "Do you attempt to play with my allegiance to cause even my men to question my word? Do you think to bring doubt and division? These here are loyal to me and have ventured at grave cost not to defy El, but to capture he that would do so. Do not compare my actions to that of my brother who had fled, FLED, to this realm that El hath named off limits. I am only here because of HIS actions; to recover again the renegade and prevent the vision given to me by thy kind of a future war that would destroy us all. Record that Grigori and never forget that it was your people who have shown me it was possible to resist the Almighty to blood itself: remember that… and fear." Michael then turned and ventured past the watery curtain to see a portal of portals. For before him was a glowing sphere that armies could march through. A portal that shimmered in plasma and from which voltage reached out like solar storms to embrace two black onyx columns that were to its right and left.

Each column towered from the floor to the ceiling, and upon each was written glyphs that were illuminated from fires that burned from within the stones themselves. A black angular chair was centered before the glowing sphere: a throne that was elevated upon a platform; and upon which was written ancient writing that was like the language of angels, but not quite Elohim.

Argoth followed in chains behind Ares and, when he saw the sight, he fell to his knees in fear. "Behold the script of God Michael. Behold the writing of God and tremble."

Michael scowled as he looked upon the Grigori as more of his men passed through the watery veil that separated the Nexus from the rest of Limbo.

The sphere then brightened several lumens higher, and plasma ejected from the great portal. Lightning strokes scratched the surface of the ceiling and let loose sparks that fell to the ground as raining embers; unleashing a smell akin to burning leaves that now filled the room.

Each angel's eyes darted to and fro, surveying the chamber;

for it was an ancient place of darkness, primordial, and raw.

The group covered their ears as a tornado-like howl filled the room. And the azure and churning portal of energy flashed and unleashed a brilliant ball of rotating plasma that catapulted from the sapphire gate. A temporal sphere of power emerged, and it dwarfed the inhabitants of the room and roared aloud its birth as it passed overhead. The temporal cyclone spit volts of lightning that collided in random and jagged lines that ripped and clawed at the surrounding area, leaving smoldering trails of its presence behind.

All watched in awe. And all eyes widened; some placed their hands over their mouths. Several of the angels that were assembled took a step backward towards the direction they had come.

Ares shook his head in concern and said, "We should not be here."

"No angel of God… you should not. You will leave now lest you raise the ire of Limbo." And the voice that spoke echoed with a tenor similar to the Ancient of Days.

The light dimmed and at the base of the throne's ascending platform were two that stood facing thirteen. One was clearly a Grigori; the other was… something else. But his eyes crackled with the same energy that emanated from the shimmering globules they had seen floating in Limbo, and which now emanated from the enormous orb above them, and from which bristled from the black spires that stood on each side of the throne. It was clear to Michael that this one was the source of Limbo's power. He who Lucifer sought help. Michael evaluated the situation and content in his assessment: spoke.

"Raphael?" Michael said warily. "Is… is that you?"

"Go back Michael… quickly and leave this place now. Leave… while you still can."

"No," said Michael. "For the renegade Lucifer sought this as a place of refuge, and thus he to your side is an aide in Lucifer's collusion to unseat El. It is clear that this seat; is a seat of power. And I claim it in the name of the Lord of Hosts: this seat of Limbo's rage. I will tame this power, control it, and I will use it to destroy any and all of Heaven's enemies."

Lotan replied, "The Tempest Throne has not been given to thee to administer. It is clear to me that you are awash in pride and act outside the station given thee. You have no power here to judge."

Michael looked down at the two men who stood at the base

but several yards from his position and replied. "Perhaps not, nevertheless… I will take it."

Michael then unsheathed his sword and several of his comrades formed to flank him: six to his right and five to his left, and they too removed their swords from their scabbards.

"You do not understand," said Lotan. "Power does not reside in the house, but in the maker of the house. Your pride has blinded you to this truth. Nor do you know with whom you speak. But foolishness hath clouded thy judgement." Lotan then moved Raphael behind him, stepped aside, and gestured with his hand that if Michael were so inclined; he might sit himself upon the throne.

Michael then smiled, walked up the platform, and sat himself upon the chair, and his hand was atop the pummel of his sword. The throne immediately responded to his presence, and light emanated from the onyx chair. The ceiling and floor flickered as arcing plasma suddenly stretched across the ceiling and began to unleash bolts of lightning that rained down upon the chamber. Raphael and Lotan watched as a sudden fog rolled across the floor from underneath them, and whispers and gaseous humanoid forms began to coalesce and take shape.

Humanoid forms and monstrosities of smoke that rose as a

ghostly army from the cavern floor.

Lotan looked at Raphael and spoke. "The angel cannot be allowed to remain on the throne or calamity will befall us all. If you wish to save your realm, yeah Creation itself, then you will dislodge him, even if it means the dissolution of your kind. For though he claims to act on El's behalf, his heart has turned already and travels a path of darkness and war. A path yet in your realm he has not made. Unseat him, destroy him if you must. But he and his company cannot abide in Limbo as their presence already stirs the Mists to feed. You must do this thing for the sake of all, for there is a greater threat that I must attend."

Raphael thought about Lotan's words and understood the gravity of the situation. He had beheld a future where El had wiped out all of creation. And Raphael knew that unless he endeavored to recapture the seat of Limbo. He was watching the beginning of the end of all things. For it was clear the Withering had descended upon Michael, and he had been in the realm too long. It was not Raphael's desire to kill his brother, nor any of his kind. But he sighed and resolved himself to do what must be done to secure Creation's survival.

Lotan, seeing Raphael's understanding on his face, then

turned to walk away.

Raphael then scrunched his face, and he remembered Lotan's words and spoke out loud. "Wait… me dislodge him?" cried Raphael. "With what do you leave to aid me? How can I defend against this company alone?"

Lotan smiled, "Fear not: for they that be with you are more than they that be with them."

Lotan then turned to depart and as he walked away, a portal appeared and he stepped through, and the portal closed behind him out of sight. Mists then began to churn along the floor and slowly coalesced into humanoid forms that formed a wall in front of Raphael and that surrounded the invading angels.

Raphael gazed upon the ghostly army that was forming before him, nodded and spoke aloud, "Very well then…" His dagger materialized in the air near his head. He took an offensive stance and made his way up the stairs of the Tempest Throne to confront an alternate version of the Prince of Kortai he knew and loved: Michael.

The Prime Realm: Henel's Past

Henel walked in blackness and when he turned behind him to see where he had entered, he saw naught but ebon. He looked at his feet and light illuminated his path. He traveled and heard whispers in the dark: whispers as of the sound of children.

"Feed the Mists," he heard the faint voices say.

"Why are you even here," said another.

Turn from this wayward path and follow us. Listen to our voice and we shall direct you towards your greatest desire."

"Who are you!" cried Henel. "Where are you!" he spoke aloud.

"We are your choices, Henel James, and we know who you are and the decisions that avail thee. Feed us, nourish us. Fatten us, for why doth thou walk a path groping in the dark when all you must do is follow our voice. Come… feed the Mists."

A light then appeared before Henel and suddenly over him was a floating Grigori not unlike Argoth save he had two faces.

"Let the human be: now away with you!" a voice commanded.

The illuminated fog then dissipated and scattered hither and thither, and Henel could see forms and shapes and legs as spiders and millipedes scamper off into the darkness, and he realized how close the creatures were to him and shuddered. He then turned to look upon the angel who assisted him and his eyes beheld the face of an angel unlike any he had ever seen.

And when the Grigori looked at him, it was with two faces, and with four eyes. And two were blazing white, set within a black face; and the others were as dark as onyx set within a white face.

"Behold the door that lies before you, human. Enter therein and know that whatever you find may not release you until a choice presents itself to be released."

Henel saw a glowing rectangle appear before him, a door of light directly in his path. He nodded to the angel and stepped into the light, and exited on the other side.

He was in a restroom.

He heard a toilet flush, and a man exited a stall and proceeded to the sink and washed his hands. Henel also rushed to wash his hands, and the man proceeded to instantly chat with him.

"Man, I am telling you that ever since the United States left the United Nations, the feed has been going off the hook. But this Lucas Alexander cat and his family character. I can't believe this family's reach into all manner of crimes; they clearly have people in their pockets and dirt on kings and politicians from every country. Anyway, I'm gonna break that cartel wide open." The man wiped his hands with some paper towel and extended his hand to shake the hand of Henel. "By the way, my name is Ezra, Ezra James you look like you're new."

Henel looked at the face of his father and stared. He had remembered as a child that his father possessed youthfulness, but now vibrant and speaking before him was the man who raised him until age sixteen, and he did all that he could to not reach out and hug him. He slowly extended his hand and shook his father's hand, as his eyes began to tear.

Ezra James lowered his eyebrows and pursed his lips. "You look a little pale there my friend, are you ok?"

Henel composed himself quickly and replied, "Yes, apparently something I ate this morning did not sit well with me."

Ezra laughed, "Ha! I'll tell anyone that will listen not to eat the breakfast menu in the cafeteria. Look, it was nice to meet you, ahh… I didn't get your name."

"Henel…"

"Henel, humph, I like that name. I've got a son named Henel. He's a sharp fella too, wouldn't be surprised if he turns out to be a journalist like his dad."

Henel choked back tears and again fought the urge to reach out and grab his father.

"Look Henel, I've got to run. But take it easy." Ezra then turned and exited the men's room and Henel listened as the door closed shut.

He slumped over the sink, and he could feel himself shaking. His breathing was rapid, and he lifted his hand to cover his mouth. He opened the tap and reached under the cool flowing water and splashed some on his face and looked at himself in the mirror.

What are you working on dad?

Henel composed himself and exited the men's room. He walked down a small hallway that opened into a large room. He paused as he surveyed the scene. He was in a group office. Various television monitors hung from the ceiling, and each display showed multiple news outlets and stock tickers that ran along the lower level of the screen. Men and women were hunched at interconnected desks, typing furiously behind computer monitors. Papers were strewn across desks and voices carried as multiple reporters were on their phones, researching stories. Men and women walked past him, heading with papers in hand to parts unknown.

The scene was a familiar one to Henel, while the newsroom was clearly outdated. He was clearly at the office headquarters of Jerusalem Post.

He found an open cubicle and sat down and turned on the monitor. He reviewed the directory options and saw that there was a communal project. Various categories raced across his screen. He then did a search for Lucas Alexander.

"Bingo," he whispered to himself.

He clicked the folder and his father's name was listed and he opened the file.

It was password protected.

Henel thought for a moment and proceeded to guess his father's passwords. He typed in various combinations when a tap on his shoulder interrupted him. He turned to see his father stare down at him, grinning.

"You know, if you wanted to know what I was working on, all you had to do was ask."

Henel flushed.

"It's alright, I saw that sparkle in your eye the moment I mentioned Lucas Alexander. If you want to learn more, follow me. Let's go to the cafe." Ezra turned to leave, and Henel quickly followed. They made themselves to the elevator and Ezra pushed the button to the first floor and the door shut them in.

"I am really sorry I don't mean to pry…"

"Please," said Ezra. "Of course, you meant to pry. But it's not an issue because Mr. Covitz has decided to not run the story."

Henel's neck drew back. "Why?"

Ezra shook his head. "Not here." Ezra's eyes then motioned upwards to the security camera that watched them. Henel nodded in understanding.

They reached the ground floor and walked to a Starbucks within the building. Grabbing their respective drinks, Ezra continued his pace outside and went around a corner into the lower garage until they came upon his parked car. He pointed his car-door opener at the vehicle and two horn chirps sounded in unison, with two flashes from his headlamps. "Get in," he said.

Henel did as bidden, and Ezra spoke.

"You look too dumb to be associated with Lucas Alexander. So, I am not going to report you. But I know you clearly don't work here. So, you spill it, and I won't inform the police."

Henel bobbed his head, "You wouldn't believe me if I told you the truth."

"Try me." Ezra said.

"I'm actually not from around here, at least not yet. But suffice it to say I am here to check on you. I don't know how much time I have, so I need to ask you a question."

"Shoot," said Ezra.

"Are you a religious man? Do you know Yeshua as Messiah and Lord?"

Ezra looked at him strangely. "No, why should I?"

Henel nodded. "Because something terrible is going to happen to you and your family. You will be shot and placed in a coma."

Ezra drew back incredulously, "Are you threatening me?"

Henel placed his hands up. "No, no… not at all. But I know that at some point something is going to happen to you and that your son Henel will go through his late teen life into adulthood missing his father. I know that whatever story you are working on will cause your wife to be killed, and that she will tell the young man that it was because of your work all, because you uncovered something. Now I do not know exactly what it is you are working on. But I can't imagine anything so important that it would cause a person to sacrifice one's family over it."

Ezra sat in his seat quietly and stared at the older man who sat across from him. He reached into his pocket and pulled out his cell phone and a USB-stick. He fiddled with the apps on his phone screen and opened a video player and set it on the middle console and pressed play.

"So, Leto held a new year's party at his flat? You say?" a voice stated.

"Yeah man, that young guy was partying hard. He was doing all kinds of women, but he loved having sex with the men in front of other men. He thought it was funny to humiliate them, you know. The kid was a sick man, just sick."

Henel could hear the voice of Ezra continuing. "Well homosexuality is a pretty normal thing these days son."

"No man, I mean this cat did what he did in front of everybody he... he..."

Henel listened and his eyes narrowed, knowing that whoever the young man was; was in distress over what he was recounting. "I came into the bedroom as he was choking him. I mean, he had him by the throat right in front of everyone. I mean, at first, we were all laughing, because you know the kid just passed out. Leto did his business, then released him and he fell like some goddamn spent up rag doll. I didn't know if it was the drugs, or what, but that cat man, that cat, was ruthless. The dude had just pleasured him in front of everyone, was just a piece of meat. It's like he saw him as a receptacle... garbage. And I'm looking at this dude. Bill was his name, yeah, and he's lying there unconscious and then we realized he was just dead... and his reaction... it was cold man."

"And what did Leto do?"

He sat down naked on a couch and took a smoke. He then asked the ten of us if we wanted to make a quick twenty-k. We were all still tripping over what we saw. Jay ran over to shake Bill up. You know, thinking he must have been pranking us... but it was no prank. He was dead, and Leto didn't care worth a crap man. "He just said if we kept silent, he'd give us twenty-k a piece."

"And did anyone ask what would happen if they didn't keep silent?" Ezra said.

"Just me, I was the only dumb shit stupid enough to ask."

"And what did Leto say?"

"He just looked at me, man, looked at me with those cold brown eyes and said, 'Well, maybe I'd have to visit your mother and see if she likes me and, more importantly, if I like her. Because if she doesn't… well, we can all see what happens when I don't like people.'

He then took out his checkbook and had us all line up and touch the body. He wanted to make sure our DNA was on the corpse in case any of us ever decided we would cross him."

"And did anyone?"

"I never thought anyone did until Jay came up missing about two weeks ago. When I asked his family about him, they said it was suicide. They found his body on the pavement in front of his flat. Police report said he jumped, and that he was depressed. But Jay wasn't a depressed man. He was planning on marrying this chick from the states. It's a lie man; a lie to cover the Alexanders."

"So, why are you telling me? Why didn't you just go to the police? Aren't you afraid for your own life?"

"Naw, man, hell, the Alexanders own the police. If I tell them, I might find myself hung dead in a cell purportedly by suicide. Besides, I'm not stupid and I ain't got no one to protect and nothing to lose. But somebody ought to know what this man did; self-righteous prick that he is. I can't believe he's slated to become an ambassador to Europe. And no man should have that kind of power to be able to kill someone all cold like that and get away with it. Jay was a good dude man, a good dude. And that Leto cat just treated him like trash. Hell, I like to party as well as the next bloke, but Jay ain't come to the party to suck dick and die, man. And when I thought about it even more, I realized that it could have been me, and what's funny is that it might have been if I didn't take that check. Chicken shit is what I was… what I am. But if I can do anything in honor of Jay's memory… his fiancé… here is the check that the rich bastard gave me. I never even cashed it. It shows the date, signature, and everything. I ain't got a lot of proof to go up against a family like that, but I have to do this. I hope the son of a bitch rots in hell."

Ezra then pushed stop on the recorder app on his phone and spoke. "The man speaking gave me this interview and this check two weeks ago. This afternoon this manila envelope was in my office mail today."

Henel took the envelope handed to him and opened it. He recoiled slightly and his mouth dropped, then turned downward in disgust, and his eyes widened. His eyes traced the features of a disfigured body that was burned. The corpse was barely recognizable. Henel saw another picture, a smaller four by six picture. It was of a woman and a small child.

His mother.

The face of Henel's mother brought back memories. The child she held hands with was the toddler version of himself at perhaps five years old. He put his hand over his mouth and his eyes tightened to hold back tears of the future he knew the message the picture was meant to convey: a message that in his reality had come to pass.

Ezra reached over and took the pictures and placed them back into the envelope.

"And you tried to run this story?"

"Henel, someone has to stop the Alexanders. Someone has to care enough to make that boy's death count. This family, Lucas and Leto, the lot of them can't be allowed to get away literally with murder and the coverup of these crimes!"

"But why you?" Henel asked.

Ezra stared at the color picture of his wife and child. "Because what kind of man, father, husband would I be if I didn't try. Whenever I looked at myself in the mirror, I'd see a coward."

Henel drew back, "But a living coward, a man who is there to see his boy grow to manhood."

"Maybe," replied Ezra. "But there is no guarantee they won't be killed just to keep me silent. They know, that I know. And it's clear that my life and that of my family are in danger. As far as I know, I'm just on borrowed time as it is. And now that I've been seen with you…"

"Now *my* life is in danger?" said Henel.

"Sorry son, but be careful when you poke around for information behind encrypted passwords and firewalls: some walls are meant to protect you."

Henel sighed and replied, "In for a penny, in for a pound. What do you need me to do? How can we stop them?"

Ezra was silent for a moment. "I'm not sure we can, but there is something that you can do to help me: and maybe strike a blow for the good guys."

"What?" asked Henel.

Ezra reached into his pocket and pulled out two plane tickets to the United States and gave them to Henel. "Go to my home; tell my wife I love her. Tell her it's time and specifically tell her that you are the 'last resort'. She will know what that means. She will want to know where you will take her. Do not tell her. Just check them in and get them on their plane. Assume you will be watched. Give her this and tell her that there is an account in her name at Chase bank from which she can draw funds. Ezra passed a handgun to Henel. "Take this and do whatever you have to do if you or their lives are in danger."

He also passed on to Henel two burner phones. "One is for you, and one is for her."

Henel took the weapon, clicked the safety to on, and then tucked the firearm into the dip of his back. Ezra nodded. "The plane leaves the tarmac at midnight. This is the address to my home."

Ezra looked at his watch and it was close to 5pm Israel Standard Time. He reached over and plugged in the address into the GPS of Ezra's car. He calculated the time needed to travel to his father's home and then to Ben Gurion Airport.

"I want you to leave immediately," said Ezra. "Here is the key to a rental." He handed Henel a key fob and clicked the right button, and the car next to theirs flickered in response. Once you arrive at the airport, there will be little anyone can do without causing a major issue with the military and the police. Sit with them until it's time. Here, take this."

Ezra reached into his breast pocket and took out a bank envelope, and passed it to Henel. Henel opened the envelope and within it were twenty-one hundred-dollar bills.

"Consider it compensation for your time," said Ezra.

"Is there anything else?" Henel asked.

"Yeah, don't get killed."

* * *

"Mr. James, are you sure my husband said those exact words?"

"Yes, ma'am." said Henel. "Those exact words. He said you would know what those mean."

Henel watched as she hurriedly packed her belongings and stuffed them into a tan suitcase.

"Henel, hurry up son! Are you ready?"

"Yes mama," came a reply from the other room. Henel watched as his younger self dragged a small suitcase down some stairs and entered the front room of the house with him and his mother.

It was an awkward experience to see his parents. The Alexanders had his mother killed not long after they traveled to America. He remembered this, but the details of her death always seemed cloudy, and out of his mind's retentive reach; but now he stood in front of his mother and feelings of anguish rushed to meet him. An internal desire compelled him to warn her about the dangers of their trip and a future to come. A future that would leave a young man orphaned.

Damn you, Janus, why did I need to see this? Why bring me here?

"I'll bring the car to the front; we need to go; we've taken too long already," said Henel. Henel rushed out of the house and as he did so fumbled with some keys to enter the vehicle and get the car started. The engine turned over quickly and the childhood version of himself sprinted out of their house. Mrs. James opened the door and placed her son in his seat and buckled him in. She, too, dashed to the passenger door and strapped herself in. "Let's go!"

Henel shifted the car into reverse and hit the gas pedal. The car acted upon command and speedily left the driveway as Henel spun the wheel to take them to Ben Gurion Airport.

"How do you know my husband?"

"Let's just say that he trusted me enough to make sure that you and your son arrive at the airport safely, and that's exactly what I am going to do."

"Will we see you again?"

Henel smiled, "Not in this lifetime, but I hope in the next."

They made their way up to the Lod Interchange without incident and then merged to the Ben Gurion interchange until the local signs directed them to departures.

He stopped the car by the side of the terminal and, with the car running, popped the trunk, got out and heaved the luggage of his mother onto the sidewalk. A porter came to assist, and he gave the man three thousand shekels. "Don't just get their luggage to the gate. Make sure they get to the gate, too. Can you do that?"

The skycap looked surprised and then replied, "If you got more than this, I'll even get with them on the plane!" He tucked the money into his vest and stood attentive to the woman that exited the vehicle with her toddler.

"That won't be necessary," replied Henel. "Just make sure they get on that plane."

"Destination?" said the Skycap.

"Air France, flight 347 to New York."

The skycap nodded and looked at Mrs. James and her boy. "Your kid?"

Henel looked at his younger self and replied, "After a fashion." He then gave his mother another 1000 shekels and spoke. "When you get through security, give this to him." He nodded to the skycap and the sky cap acknowledged he had more to earn if he successfully completed his mission.

Henel then hugged his mother in a long embrace and sniffed her hair. "I miss you." He whispered.

She pulled away from him and stared at him, and she lifted young Henel into her arms to protect him. "Who are you?"

Henel was silent, and the skycap interrupted their awkward pause, "If you would like to follow me, ma'am."

He took their luggage cart and wheeled it into the terminal. As she entered the airport, Mrs. Abigail James looked back to see

59

Henel get into her car. She stared at the man; then her eyes narrowed as a waxing recognition befell her mind that she watched her adult son drive off.

*　*　*

Henel drove back onto the expressway that would lead him back into the city. His thoughts fluttered as a bird over his mind until the situation could no longer be tolerated, and he pulled over and wept.

He banged his hands on the steering wheel and screamed in rage. Rage because he knew the outcome of his decision to drop his mother off at the airport. She would indeed arrive in New York and for about a year, all would seem well. Until one night he would see a man, his face covered with pantyhose, standing over his mother with a gun in hand. And his mother sprawled out on the floor, dead execution style. He would recall the screams for "momma" that lifted from his throat, and the rage that would well into him to attack his mother's murderer: a man that would never be identified. A man whom he would attack, and with his black leather-gloved hand; would back-hand him into unconsciousness.

Again, he bashed his hands into the steering wheel and the horn blared in reaction to his displeasure.

With a grimaced face, he spoke aloud. "No, I can stop it. It does not have to be this way."

He pressed his foot to the gas pedal, and the car peeled back onto the road. He found a service way and turned back towards the airport. Rubber tires gripped the asphalt road as black tread marks left their shadow on the pavement. The odometer spiked past the legal speed limit until it reached 100 km/h.

Henel now raced back towards the airport; having decided to undo what had already been done. And with his heart now settled upon his choice, the azure blue of limbo emblazoned over his car and saturated the cabin until the man re-materialized, running through the darkness. The dread fog of Limbo was as a river of smoke about his feet and parted as he slowed his gait in exhaustion, and then finally his run. Henel panted, catching his breath as the angel Janus stood before him with two faces and stared into the eyes of the human. Henel fell to his knees and his head swayed in sad resignation that he was helpless to undo the events of the past and tears welled up in his eyes. And he looked up into the cold and empty eyes of the two faced Grigori and spoke.

"What was I supposed to do... let her die?"

Janus looked down upon the man and his cloak swayed in the small breeze that wafted through Limbo. "Redaction of this journal is forbidden."

Henel's mouth was down turned, and he choked on his words. "Of course, it is." And he gripped the porous earth in his hands and wept.

The Prime Realm: The Ancient Past

El sat quietly upon his throne. He watched from the Mercy Seat the happenings of the universe and eyed the seeds of rebellion slowly taking root in Lucifer. He pondered in silent contemplation while observing Michael's innocence being stripped away: innocence eroded by the exposure to new truths his Creator knew he could no longer shield from him.

El understood that free-will brought with its creation risk: but a risk the Creator was willing to take. For before the foundation of the world, El had anticipated the possible paths that free will could take with his creations. Thus, El explored the multiple branches that would spring from the first deviation from God's will. A deviation that would not remain contained within one species of creation but go viral into another, causing the eventual decay of the whole.

But to withhold his grand design to create something other than God would not be denied. To not create was not an option. Thus, El had indeed anticipated this occurrence and understood the suffering that would result in bringing life into the world. Nevertheless, God would allow for the existence of conscience: allow for the curious thing called free-will and the freedom to pursue life apart from Him and to instead embrace death. Nor would he, for the sake of love, or convenience, inhibit this choice. The capacity to experience true fellowship could not be denied.

And the Creator of all things sighed within himself as he pondered how much easier to create sentience with no conscience: instinct with no morality. No ability to extend love as love was given by the Creator. But God would not shrink from pain but open himself up to injury, sadness, and grief. He would sorrow with his creation and rejoice when it rejoiced. All to see his own love reflected to him in another.

And though God could choose to remain alone: to sustain himself on himself and to live as the eternally existent one without anyone; such was not El's way. For goodness itself had determined that it was not good that God should be alone, and therefore, El made angels to stand in his presence. And when the first was brought into existence, El willed there would be another. And determined to fashion from the mud another agent with conscience and yea even his image and would breathe into him the breath of life. Yea, he would mold another he could love, and who could appreciate the wonder of a world made just for him. And God would walk with him, and they would fellowship one with another. El knew it was an audacious plan and daring in design to create a race of beings that could one day rise to hate their creator. But God is love and love compelled the Lord to act.

"Do you reminisce, father?"

The familiar voice of Yeshua was heard as El turned his head to see his only begotten son standing, looking at him lovingly. "There is much that transpires in Limbo. For even now Jerahmeel stands in the basement of Heaven to defy the Mists entry into the land whilst Michael and Gabriel rally the Lumazi to assist him. And in between the crevices we have made in time and space; the Grigori fight with members of the Host against the embryo of a prison I have prepared for the devil and his angels."

Yeshua looked at the Father, smiled and replied, "But ah Lord God, thou who hast made the heavens and the earth by thy great power and by thy outstretched hand: surely they will find their way. This path that we tread, have we not purposed to allow it; that we might have fellowship?"

El looked upon the devastation and watched as even the human Henel James traversed the corridors of time that was Limbo. "The thing is as you say."

"Face it father, for you long to save, you who are long suffering in mercy. And though they stir you up to strife and give cause for thee to destroy all things. We both know that I will stand as the lightning rod of thy wrath and bear the brunt of their foolishness and sin that we all one day might have fellowship. We have committed ourselves to this path. And lo, yet I know it is one thing to see the suffering in our mind's eye: I too am burdened to hear the screams, pain, and cries of those not yet even born. But I AM that I AM. And we shall endure this purging and remove the dross from both conscience and free-will until all that remains is love of God and love of brother. Therefore, I pray thee, father; interfere not, let this path play itself out, though it be hard for us to bear. Know that I will not shrink from the burden you would place on me."

El nodded. "It shall be as you say. And though their sins be as scarlet, I shall make them white as snow."

Yeshua and El then turned their heads at once towards the sky. Their eyes seeing past gold and marble ceilings and into the Aerie home of the Ophanim. For the nest of the celestial creatures were stirred, and they moved in agitation; for they were aware of the goings-on of Limbo. And Eladrin, the King of the Ophanim, turned, and the sky turned with him. And constellations moved at his command and solar systems coordinated their circuit around the galaxies at his agitated turning.

His bird-like eyes looked to the palace of Heaven and locked eyes with the Father and Son. And upon their glance; solace filled the heart of Eladrin, and the King bowed as only a wheel within a wheel could, and thoughts of peace flooded his heart, for the Lord was there. The Ophanim saw past the throne of the Lord and peered deep within the bowels of the palace into the basement of the mountain. Eladrin watched as one angel battled ancient forces stirred to span a barrier not meant to be crossed by their kind; ethereal shadows of the deep confined to a realm of darkness: the awakened and growing wraiths of sentience contrary to God. And for a moment his heart raced, and galaxies shuddered for his trembling.

Eladrin then sensed a presence manifest to his rear, and the still small voice of the Holy Spirit spoke aloud. "Peace Eladrin. Be still and know that I am God."

Eladrin then crooned a song of peace to his people, and the Ophanim stilled themselves and waited quietly for the Holy Spirit to speak once more. And the Spirit of the Living God crooned to his creation.

El sat quietly on his throne and waited for events he had set in motion to play out. Events that he knew would one day pit his angelic sons against him and force his hand to save mankind from the wiles of the Devil: events that one day would lead even to the death of God.

* * *

Lucifer Chi moved with sword drawn to bring down the forces arrayed against him. His voice was a sonic scythe that cut down carrion after infernal carrion that was birthed from the womb of the strange underground mountain.

For deep within the bowels of this land, Lucifer seemed to experience the sensation of prescience. An overwhelming sensation that plagued him that while he was here, that he would in the future be here… but not here in this location or even this time. An uneasy awareness enveloped him that he was reliving, or perhaps soon would experience a future where he would fight a living creature of earth and stone: something similar but different. Yet in his unease, there was comfort that he was not alone, for Michael fought by his side. And the angel turned to see his brother, who he found to his rear protecting his hind.

There was a sense of security in his presence. A comfort in knowing that if he stood with his brother by his side, there was nothing he could not face; nothing they could not tame; for they were imbued with the power of El and walked with his authority wherever their paths took them. Surely there was no foe, real or imagined, that could bring them low. For El was their sword and shield. And they were on a mission of righteousness to bring together what El had never meant to be sundered: to restore the unity of the spirit of the angelic houses.

Lucifer watched the scene before him; cognizant that many of his fellows were overwhelmed and would not return to the capital city. Doubt crept into his mind. A sliver of uncertainty that perhaps the path he had trodden was not to confront Grigori and bring them home. He wondered to himself that perhaps it was hubris that brought them all here. The hubris to think that anyone might defy him, the chief of angels. Was he not the most beautiful of El's creations, not the epitome of angelic wisdom and strength? Yet Raphael and his kind turned their backs on his leadership, beauty, and wisdom. Instead, a cohort of angels had elected to separate themselves from the association of the Parliament of angels: all to be away from him.

How can such an offense be allowed?

And amid the battle, Lucifer searched himself to see what lies underneath. To determine if the will of El was what drove him. Or something deeper he had yet to understand.

I am as God. He thought.

It was an occasional thought that rose to the surface of his mind. For the Creator leaned on him to convey his word and to promote his works. To lean upon the service of his creation implies that El saw Lucifer as a pillar upon which he could support his weight: a pillar that the God of the Universe could rest on. Lucifer was proud of this revelation. This knowledge he had come into by his own imagination. And what need was there to dialogue with El to confirm this belief? Was it not clear for all to see?

What need he query the Lord as to the veracity of this logic? For was it not self-evident in El's constant errands? Was the thing not known among the Elohim, and among the Seraphim and even the Ophanim.

It was a strange thing to know the Creator depended upon you. For it could mean but one thing. That perhaps God was not omnipotent. Perhaps… there was a need that only the Elohim could fulfill? A need that Lucifer himself was alone sufficient?

Perhaps it was even possible to be God. For if God himself leaned upon Lucifer to complete the tasks of the Creator, perhaps all creation could be benefited from his leadership? Lucifer allowed his mind to germinate on the idea and he turned it over in his thoughts to come to but one conclusion. "I should be God."

Flaming carrion rose and attempted to accost him, to no avail. For Lucifer was the arm of the living God, and his power could bring Creation to ruin, if he were to wish it so.

"Are you alright, brother?" said Michael.

Lucifer nodded. "We cannot maintain this position; we must seek means to achieve superiority in this battle. I will not have us stalemated in our efforts. Find those of the Grigori who lead their house, find them, brother, and we must fight as one to beat back this threat. Now hurry and go about my business."

Michael nodded and launched himself into the air to attend to the words of his brother.

Lucifer looked at Michael as he flew off to find the heads of house Grigori and wondered if he should share with Michael his thoughts on his being God when this was over.

Perhaps at some point we would share his mind… perhaps. Perhaps explain his righteous ambition to achieve a status unknown by angelic kind: a status to be as God himself.

* * *

Michael Chi flew over the moving mountain. It lumbered along the floor of Limbo and left a long trail of dredged out earth. It was clear the creature moved towards a direction that would send it to the Nexus. Michael observed the battles from above and concluded the creature's intent was not to simply attack them, but to travel towards the center of the land of Limbo.

What manner of creature is this, that it would be drawn towards the midway of Limbus?

Perhaps the Nexus should be investigated more than rallying the leaders of Grigori to assault the creature?

The Chief Prince continued his ruminations. For while he

loved his brother, from the moment Lucifer announced his plan to compel House Grigori by force, he was uneased. Who but the Lord could authorize such an act? Yet here in the depths were the host trespassing in a realm deemed off limits by El. For now, thousands of Heaven's companies led by but one; were engaged in battle. Michael could not help but weigh his own actions. Could not help but cringe that he too had fallen prey to the mass delusion that to defy El's word would not be without consequence.

"Lord God, please forgive me."

Michael then turned from the path directed by Lucifer to search out the heads of the Grigoric forces and instead looked to the path that the beast lumbered towards the Nexus.

The head of House Kortai set his face to the center of Limbo to seek a solution that might save them all.

The Nexus: The Ancient Past

Argoth watched as Raphael approached the Tempest throne and a wall cloud of mist ascended with him; a fog that churned to hide within its vaporous cloak, monstrous faces, and mouths of fangs that whispered indecipherable words: a menacing ethereal guard that stood adjacent on each flank of the angel.

Michael stared, unimpressed, and simply motioned with his hand. Immediately, two of his men stepped grudgingly forward. They eyed the Mist and the menace that moved within its shadow and then unsheathed their swords.

Raphael then paused, and the wall cloud also stopped its advance.

"It is not my desire to destroy you, High Prince; nor my desire to engage my brethren. I will ask you, but once more, to yield this seat of power. Only one from House Grigori can control the Tempest Throne. Transgress no longer and all will be well. Continue in your actions and know that I will not spare your life."

Argoth watched while he was held bound and heard Michael's muffled reply, but his attention was distracted and a faint buzzing beckoned him to turn his head and lift his ear rearward. He noted the floor illuminated with pulses of light that raced along the ground, while each spire that towered to the thrones left and right brightened and bathed the cathedra in a bluish glow.

Michael rose from the chair and the pulses raced the more. But Argoth saw that the High prince and his men were focused on Raphael and the ominous smog before them and not the developing sight to their rear and that none seemed aware of the buzz, at least at first.

Small rocks then lifted from the ground and stirred dust fell from the massive cavern as sprinkled snow. The low buzz turned into a growling rumble that could be felt in the ground and caused several of those assembled to lose their balance and trip over their own feet. The circular gate that hovered above the throne then sprung to life awash in pearly light, and it was then that all turned to see multiple arcs of lightning leap from the onyx spires to the left and right of the throne and burst in elongated tendrils to grip one another in rising electrified cords into the cavern sky.

Light ejected forth from the gate in blinding fury, and Argoth shouted what all knew was now forthcoming.

"Temporal Storm!"

The gate belched and unleashed what the eye could only describe as ball lightning. Yet, Argoth could see visions within the now developing and twirling storm; images of alternative possibilities that churned and wrestled for dominance; a dominance to be the prime reality from a host of brawling multitudes and to reach out and transform the landscape: to craft from a multiplicity of possibilities: a reality of one. The schizophrenic time-lines raged in fury and a ball of blue green rotating light jettisoned from the onyx gate that hovered above the throne. And all looked on in horror, for the gate was as a temporal trebuchet carrying a reality warping payload: now targeted to destroy them all.

Chi Realm: The Ancient Past

Lotan left Raphael's side and materialized at the basement of Heaven. He walked up the stairwell to enter the palace grounds. Veiled from the sight of angelic eyes, his presence did not go undetected from his own people. Dozens of grigori looked upon him with eyes raised, while others paused in their recording of events in surprise as he walked by. All that saw him turned their eyes towards him, and all that beheld him bowed to show respect.

For before them all floated the father of their order and the first grigori ever given a charge. But his was unique in that he was to wait until the Lord gave word to write. Then would his pen write. But for now, Lotan's pen was silent. For House Grigori knew what the rest of the royal houses did not: that Lotan's pen would be the one to redact, not to record. Thus the father of Grigori floated unmolested into the palace; all thinking that El had summoned the angel for a personal audience. The palace was a massive structure built into the mountain of God and was something the angel had not seen in person in many of Heaven's days. And yet today was not a day he could permit himself to enjoy the sights and sounds of the capital city. Today was a day he must find Lilith of House Grigori, and stop him if able from unleashing destruction upon them all. Lotan had seen the possibilities that might bring him into the palace. He had seen a vision of an angel walk into his realm at the command of the Sephiroth, only to be changed into the Sephiroth himself.

His mission was not to just prevent destruction but to rescue a unique Elohim by the name of Janus, who was like him but also a two-faced one and able to see past and future. Janus could no longer remain in any realm save Limbus. Only El, in his providence and sovereignty, had allowed the transformation of Janus into the Book of Life.

Today, he must find Janus. Lotan entered the palace unencumbered and followed the energy trail of the Sephiroth that was Janus. For Lotan could see the image of his peer: this being who was like him and destined to one day guard the realms of creation from those within and to prevent those without. Lotan had seen this possibility, this future, and the development of Janus' life was indeed following the course he had envisioned. And the father of House Grigori continued in his musings as he winded down various hallways of the palace and corridors. His anxiety growing that while he had seen Janus's possible future. Nowhere had he seen his own. And he prayed silently to himself and reached out to his God.

El, I too now stand on one side of Limbo, subject to the gift of choice. My story now interwoven into the tale that will be this present. For I no longer stand atop the Tempest Throne. No longer am I in the realm of choices as arbiter; but in this realm… this possibility. I pray you will honor thy servant's service to bring to fruition what I know is thy desire. For how can I allow thine wrath to go unabated? For, though thou hast permitted me to see the fates of others, but my predestination is now hidden from me. But know, oh God, that I accept the will of my Lord and, like all, serve my Creator. Heed my prayer, my king. And give thy servant success and let not thy hot wrath wax and lead to the consumption of all things.

Lotan surprised himself with his prayer. For his destiny was to usher in the Void: to undue at the command of God all things; to be the realm in between the upcoming new heaven and new earth. His work would see the erasure of the old to make way for the new. But Lotan found himself enjoying this reality: spending time with his kind. Yet, he understood his purpose: to observe from the Tempest Throne. To watch and witness, as was the lot of all Grigori that followed him. But here in the capital, his interactions with Raphael, Argoth and even Michael revealed an awareness he did not truly possess prior: a lifting of the veil of his eyes that he was alone. A celestial voyeur unable to enjoy the pleasure of fellowship, and the thought plagued him that he wanted more. And he was careful to not covet what other Elohim had: fellowship.

He came to the end of his journey through the palace and saw the signature of Janus through a door. He placed his hand upon the handle and stepped through and what he saw was as he had seen in the seeing orbs of Limbus.

For Lilith held Janus bound and a floating pedestal held a book whose pages were also floating from Janus to form its growing volume.

"Hail son of Grigori," said Lotan. "You who have been sired of my house. Be not afraid… yet. For though you have hidden thyself in another reality, I cannot be escaped, nor is the hand of El short that he cannot touch thee. Know that I have come for the book and he whom thou hast bound with thy magics. Cease in this way and allow for restoration. Continue and know that you defy the King of the Tempest Throne."

Lilith eyed him, who had mysteriously entered the space with him, and replied. "What you ask I cannot do and who you seek, I cannot give. For I have seen a vision: a vision dreadful. An image I cannot unsee and that compels me now."

"There is no vision that warrants this action," said Lotan. "For, I have seen thee from afar off. And have watched as you slipped between the folds of my realm. I have observed how you have used the stolen God-stone to provide thee passage between dimensions and to peer with no Godsight into timelines, not your own. For you have entered and seen the forbidden and have traversed the circle of time, and for all thy acts, for all thy mischief, what son of Grigori did your wanderings show you?"

Lilith looked at Lotan and replied, "That in no realm, am I alive: in no time do I exist after the secession of angels. I have foreseen the fall of Lucifer, and the exile of angels. I have traversed deep into the future and have seen mankind run amok as a pestilence upon the earth. Yea, I have even seen Argoth in the future: the Sephiroth from my realm. But how is that possible? For, there cannot be two Sephiroth. But above all, in no future was the name Lilith heard on the tongues of the living."

Lotan stared at Lilith in silence, then walked to Janus, who lay unconscious on the stone slab. He felt the straps that restrained him, and the bindings that were a part of his flesh.

"To do this Lilith…to tamper with the Book of Life. To read the angst of God, and to know if thy name resides in the Yeshua's Book of Life, will not bring resolution to your pre-destined demise." Lotan looked at Janus as he slept and stroked his head. "This one here is apprehended by me to assist in the ministration of Limbus. You cannot have him. And I require his release. You must stop this madness now."

Lilith looked at the two and replied. "Be not angry with thy servant. For, thou art the father of our house and to thee I make my appeal. For you have power over the Nexus, to alter time itself. For this I know…I understand who you are. You are the steward to the realm of choices. Thus, I ask of thee, are there no pathways of choice open from the future that awaits me?"

Lilith looked at Lotan pleadingly, but all that he could see were eyes that were an absorbing white, and pupils that were wells of nothing, swallowing infinity.

"Who I am cannot change the course of the decisions you have made. Your actions have reverberated within Limbo itself and have drawn my attention: even now your sin has manifested as a fresh vapor that grows the Mists. Your actions, even now, nourish the shadows of sin. This is something that you have genesised, and a fruit of which you must bear. For the wages of sin is death. And to alter this law is not within my power to curtail. If you release this one here. I will do what I can to mitigate your fate, but if you persist… know that El will release a fury that will result in the oblivion of all things. And all you would have wrought is to cause the living to suffer for thy decisions. For thou and all Elohim are kilned from stone. Only man is from the dust of the ground. He is but clay and malleable in the hands of the Almighty. But alas, we are not so; our choices once made cannot be undone. They are petrified upon the Book of Life nor forgiven by the remission of blood."

Lotan walked towards Lilith and the rogue angel averted his eyes and backed away.

"You will release Janus, and undue the magic that you have unleashed to his harm," said Lotan.

Lilith continued walking backwards until he stumbled over the podium that held Janus's floating heart of a book.

He pulled himself up and looked to Lotan, "And what of I? Will there be no more choices for this one? Has my race run its course?"

Lotan eyed Lilith and replied, "There may be one way yet to undo thy destiny; another option to start thy choices anew. But it is a narrow path. Commit thy way to me and cede from this path and I will use the power of Limbus to alter thy path and perchance give thee avenue to start anew."

Lilith nodded his head and moved his hands over the stone. The beryl colored gem crackled in power. Green tendrils already wrapped around the tome pulsated in rapid succession.

Janus shook his head, and his breathing became rapid and his mouth opened with a guttural scream.

Lotan looked at his peer, then at Lilith, and spoke, "Know that if he dies; any chance that you seek for restoration dies with him."

"I know, I know!" cried Lilith. "The stone is not responding to my commands. It is as if something is attempting to siphon its power... something else is exerting control!"

Lotan looked at the floating heart of Janus, and then at the straps embedded in his skin: each representative of the seals which bound the Book of Life.

A seal then snapped.

Janus lifted his head and screamed.

Lotan's eyes shifted to Janus as he watched his flesh cauterize before him. The sizzling of the seal wafted the stench of burning flesh into his nostrils and a charcoal-like burn mark was now seared over the angel's chest.

A flash of light emanated from the Book of Life and a shock wave sprinted towards them both, knocking each of them down. The pulse shattered the stained glass windows of the room and left cracks that crept along the walls of the room.

Both Lilith and Lotan turned from Janus, who weakly raised his finger to point at his floating heart. For rising from within the book was a figure of a man upon a white horse and he that sat upon him had a white bow; and a crown was upon his head: and he looked menacingly at the duo and smiled at Janus, who fainted at the sight. And written upon the crown of the man was a language that Lotan had seen in the far future: a language that mankind would one day call 'Latin'.

"In hoc signo vinces" were the words that floated in the smoke of the which roughly translated in the Latin tongue, In this sign thou shalt conquer.

And upon his head was written a name that also translated

into a number. And Lotan turned to grab Lilith by the arm and he lifted him up to see how his work summoned this being that was an abomination: a being that had the number 666 printed on both his forehead and in the palm of his hand. A being who Lotan had seen in the future and one born out of time: a Nephilim and a child of Lucifer's making who held the power to siphon Elomic life and bred to challenge the Almighty: the Antichrist.

Prime Realm: Distant Past

Batriel remembered when he had first seen Jerahmeel use his power over the elements. A God given ability to slow ye, even stop the motion of atoms: freezing what he willed. He remembered as he watched Jerahmeel project cold into creation to create the most amazing of structures and release winter on multiple planets. He had observed that it was even possible for the prince to shatter the ice creations he had made. Batriel watched as the former structures collapsed on themselves, but it was the sound of their destruction that had fascinated him as a Grigori; for the sound was akin to the shattering of paned glass that fell as rain from the sky. And now the crinkling and exploding sounds echoed against the walls. The impact of freshly smattered mists reverberated through the floors and walls and Batriel watched as his charge fought an army of ghostly apparitions alone. For, with hammer and axe, Jerahmeel shattered the icy and solidified forms of creatures born out of the encroaching mists. Creatures, when destroyed, collapsed as demolished crystals to the ground below.

And Batriel was faithful to pen the destructive exertions of Jerahmeel. For he remembered when the angel was gifted his hammer and axe by Ares. And had watched as he practiced against straw dummies in its use. He even recorded Jerahmeel's guffaw over the need for such a tool. And recalled the angel outwardly questioning the wisdom for such equipment. "Who stands as opposition against the Elohim, that I need to yield a… what did you call this device… a weapon?"

Ares replied, "Aye, and chide me not, for El has commissioned me himself to create, therefore create I do. I do not question the wisdom of my God. Perhaps there are enemies afar off the God-king sees? Perhaps a foe that may be nearby? Alas, it is not my lot to question the mind of God. I have smithed and given thee the weapon as ordered by El. Do not shame me for obeying my God."

Batriel noted Jerahmeel bowed in recognition of the service done to him and for many a day the weapons stayed quiet and were sheathed along the arch of Jerahmeel's back. Tucked away for a purpose not yet revealed. But today, Batriel saw firsthand the deadly nature of the blades and destructive power the weapons could unleash when their wielder was roused to destroy.

Footsteps scurried from outside the vestibule of Limbo.

Batriel turned his head away towards the sound of hurried and multiple feet and the flap of wings that descended to the area that Jerahmeel fought to hold. Grigori's eyes could see through the wall that separated him and those who had come to give Prince Jerahmeel aid.

Michael, Gabriel, Talus, Sariel rushed down the ancient stairwell into the basement of Heaven and came to the door that was the entrance to the antechamber that led to Limbus.

Each eyed that the door was shut and iced over as if cold itself were alive as a vine and had crept along the contours of the door and seeped in between crevices of the ancient wood that held the entryway together.

Michael tugged at the door, but it held fast. He frowned, then took his shoulder and rammed it against the door and yet it still held against the high prince's might. He then placed his ear against the door and listened.

The muffled cries and exertion of Jerahmeel could be heard from within the corridor that led to Limbo.

"I am the standard of the Living God! And the shield of Heaven's shore. Though a thousand crash against me, know that I shall not be moved!"

Michael turned his head, looked at Talus, and spoke. "Bring it down."

Talus moved to the front of the group and eyed the door. He then lifted his foot into the air and kicked at the wooden entrance.

Wood boards splintered, unable to hold against the force of the Arelim's blow. Again, Talus punched and kicked at the door; he pulled beams of ancient shittim wood from its foundations and tore at the headers as splinters and shards of sculpted timber flew behind him. All watched him and then gawked as the debris cleared to reveal what lay behind the door as Talus stepped back to see his handiwork.

Mouths of the group dropped; for, behind the door was a wall of translucent ice at least an angel's body length thick. And they all could see the shadowy figure of Jerahmeel swinging his axe and hammer at… at… something. But what was evident was that Jerahmeel had barred himself from escaping from the adversary he fought… but also barred help from reaching him. The realization that the High Prince of House Harrada had confined himself to mayhap die within an icy tomb of his own making gripped them all. But it was Michael who mouthed the words that all present pursed their lips to speak.

"My God Jerahmeel, what have you done?"

And Batriel the Grigori appointed to Prince Jerahmeel was

faithful to record all that was seen.

Act II

Chi Realm: The Ancient Past

A man with the white crown stepped down from his horse and tucked his bow behind his back. His eyes narrowed, and he scanned his surroundings to see where he was.

Lotan shoved Lilith behind him. But there was nothing he could do with Janus. For he was still laid bound upon the table, strapped and semi-conscious.

The Antichrist beheld a book hovered over a pedestal, and he floated towards it, then his feet came to rest on the stone floor.

He eyed the book, then turned his gaze toward the angel Janus who was splayed out upon a stone table and who shook his head from side to side as with a fever and spoke in unintelligible gibberish. The Anti-Christ then cocked his head and walked over to where Janus lay and looked at him, and spoke.

"Who am I?"

Janus's eyes grew wide in horror, and he opened his mouth to reply, but his response was gibberish to the man.

He grabbed Janus by his cheeks and held him tight. "I know that I have a name and the word rattles in my mind… I am called… Leto. And you creature… you know me… yes?"

Again, nothing but gibberish flowed from Janus's mouth and tears welled from his eyes, as he continued to shake his head from side to side.

"Argggghh!!!" cried Janus. And virtue left the angel as his features aged and slowly withered while Leto touched him.

"Hear me!" roared the Antichrist. His hand began to glow, and he withdrew them to gaze upon them. Power rippled through his palms, and he opened and closed his hands into fists. "I feel... stronger." He then looked upon Janus once more and reached out to grab his face.

Janus cried aloud and gazed upon the man, then shouted in agony two words. "Abomination... Nephilim!"

Leto released the angel's face and staggered back as if someone had struck him. "I know this name."

Janus's yelps grew quiet, and he fell into unconsciousness.

"Leave him be!" cried a voice to the man's rear.

Leto turned towards the speech and saw two angels. One stood as if to protect and guard the other, and both held daggers drawn and raised high, ready to strike at him.

"Ah, someone who I presume knows something," said Leto. "Tell me, creature. Where am I? And why do you shield this one here from me? Who am I that I would pose a threat to you? I sense the fear hovering over you as an odiferous odor. It wafts as a cloud over you and gives me pause. Tell me what is this… abomination that he speaks of? What is Nephilim? Tell me I do not wish to do you harm."

Lotan replied, "Your presence is harm enough. Your very existence is an abomination. You are wine mixed with water, the dross of a creation never meant to be."

Leto Alexander, Anti-Christ, and Nephilim walked closer towards them. Lotan pushed Lilith to his rear and stood to engage Leto. But not before the sounds of crackling lightning emanated from where Janus lay. Leto turned to see that a black globule of light shimmered in a green glow, and a book rested on a dais and hovered. Light rose over Janus's chest and several illuminated straps could be seen embedded within his flesh. Leto rushed to the dais and gripped the stone. Waves of temporal power flowed over him, and then… into him. He absorbed the emerald gems' energy and the light which illuminated from Janus dimmed and then grew dark, and the portal that had opened closed.

"He drains the Kilnstone." whispered Lilith. "He has siphoned its power somehow."

Lotan watched as Janus' features wrinkled and the seals which pulsated were now quiet.

"I have memories from this one here. This… Janus knows your name; knows your title. He and you are called Sephiroth.

You are… Lotan: firstborn of House Grigori, Keeper of the Tempest Throne. This place, I am in the Temple of the Living God…" Leto held the stone in his hands, and it disintegrated into dust. He walked slowly towards Lotan, and his eyes narrowed as he spoke.

"I am aware, aware now, to know that I have seen the future contained behind the eyes of this one here. I have seen that I am destined to live an eternity in a lake of fire. That I am sired from an angel named Lucifer: an angel who has warred with God. That I am but an instrument designed to be used to strike at the Creator. I am a weapon, but I have now closed these seals. I will allow no additional incursion to cause my contention with the God-king to be interfered with. And you Lotan, Head of your angelic house, will aid me."

Lotan's neck jerked back in disbelief, "I will never raise my hand against El, and never will I assist thee in insurrection against my king."

Leto smiled, "You speak under the false impression that you have a choice angel." Leto walked towards Lotan. "Believe me when I say you do not."

Lotan then raised his dagger into the air, "And you are under the false impression that your covetousness will leave you unscathed."

Lotan then lunged towards Leto and, with the downward

stroke of his dagger, plunged it into the shoulder of the Nephilim. The Antichrist winced in pain and let out a guttural cry. But Leto grabbed Lotan by the neck and would not let go. And it was then that a smile came over him and Lotan realized too late the mistake he had made.

"Foolish angel, only now do you realize the error of your ways. El was wise to wipe my kind from existence. But it will not avail him now… not when I have you."

And in the moments that the words had left Leto's mouth, virtue left Lotan, and he could feel the life force from El leaving his body, and he watched in horror as the wound just inflicted on the half-man, half-angel; healed itself before his eyes: horror as he attempted to raise his hands to force the release of Leto's hold, only to see his hands wrinkle and grow gaunt.

"You possess the power to portal," said Leto. "And now I will use this power to aid me. To transport me to the place you have tried to shield in your mind's eye but cannot be hidden from me. But you are more than transportation: more than even this one upon the stone table: you are the key to the… yes… Tempest Throne, and the means to unleash my essence in all realities. Thank you, angel, for with this power of the Void I will bring Lucifer, Creation and the Godking to his knees. Yes, thank you for this knowledge, and as your reward, I will leave you alive. I will return for you in time to share with me the other secrets you have; indeed, perhaps I will have use for you in my Kingdom to come."

A portal then opened that crackled with electricity and shimmered to show the Nexus in the distance. A fog crept into the room from the celestial doorway.

"Withdraw," said Leto. "It is not yet time to consume… not yet."

Immediately the fog whispered in voices, barely perceptible and did as commanded and withdrew back within the realm of Limbo.

Leto then dropped Lotan to the ground and turned when he eyed Lilith cowering in a corner.

"Do not be afraid. Come here, angel. I wish to give you a gift. For I see that you also have seen your future and desire to escape. Come to me and I will assure you a future that may allow you to avoid the death that we both know is sure to come. Come and let me bestow upon you what Lotan would withhold."

Lilith looked at Lotan and Janus. Janus was slowly coming to, but Lotan sat prone on the floor, wheezing from the drain of power taken by the Anti-Christ. Lilith's lips then turned downward, and he trudged towards the Nephilim and then bowed his head.

"Good," said Leto. "For all shall bow soon. But I shall note that you are the first. And as promised, I bestow upon you a gift."

Leto then reached and placed the palm of his hand upon Lilith's forehead and spoke. "My essence, I pass to you. With the laying of my hands, I transfer my essence that will survive attempts to see you undone. An essence that will, in time, be a seed that will grow and a harvest if I am denied. The essence of my father I pass to you. The future of his son you now bear, and the fruit of which will assure my inevitable return should things go awry. For I have seen the future and I go to assure our own."

A portal then appeared behind Lilith, and Leto lifted his hands from atop Lilith's head. And Lilith wondered over the words spoken over him, as Leto walked past him into the shimmering portal to parts unknown and vanished from his sight.

And Lotan, having witnessed the exchange of words and deeds, opened his mouth even as Lilith rose to his feet.

"You know not what you have done, and you have doomed yourself and Heaven to incur a civil war that will play out over an eon." He then tilted his head; heavy from weakness and a tear welled up in his eye as he pondered in disbelief the events now unfolding.

"In El's name, Lilith… what have you done?"

The Prime Realm: The Ancient Past

In the deep realms of Heaven, the creature Hell walked the grounds of Limbo. Her entrails dragged behind her craggy body and her intestines belched fire and brimstone. She was a living mound of rock and sulfur, fueled by the vengeance of God. Pain was something unknown to this creature, for she was the purveyor of pain, the living domain that would one day house the unrighteous dead. She was primordial and premature in consciousness of the things around her. Undeveloped and awakened before her time, but above all things… she was enraged.

Like a tantrum thrown by a newborn babe that hungers. So, too, did Hell cry her displeasure: a wailing pyrotechnic mix of sulfur, ash, and fire. The steaming hiss of Sheol's breath, coupled with the crackling sound of burning flesh, rose into the ceiling of Limbo into the ears of all. It was a ballad of animalistic and volcanic grunts mixed with the screams of angels burned alive: angels who dared cross the fledgling mountain. Rocky tentacles raised themselves into the air, only to smash down upon the bodies of angels who had assembled to stop her. Her starfish-like movement made her lumber over the rocky gravel that was the basement of Heaven. As thousands of angels assailed craggy feet who, in their audacity, sought to slow her in her snail-like march. For, even in this infant stage, she was aware of the vain attempts to bring her to heel. But they were parasites to be consumed by the rocky amoeba. And like a pseudopod, she extended herself to pull angels within her to be digested and to consume all things alive.

She hungered, and angel flesh was the nourishment that sustained her. And as a mother feeds from her breast, so too did Limbo provide from her bosom the milk of Elomic life. And the wide fiery maw of Hell's mouth sought to latch upon all that Limbus offered.

The angels that flew and crashed against her did not move her. No, all they did was loosen from their mouths the unintelligible screams she was acclimating herself to hear as she fed. For hers was to know that such were the calls to feast and knowing that her prey was sentient mattered not; that they loved, hated, or chose mattered not: nothing mattered save her hunger. Thus, she was mindful only of her need to feed and to the outside world that fed it.

Her rocky shell concealed raging fires within and with each digestion of an angel; worms were created that sought in flames life that might serve as compost to aid her growth; fuel to fire her fires and enlarge her mass. Ever moving, ever raging, she was a sure coming punishment to all that would one day find themselves outside the love of God.

The final destination for the wages of sin.

It was then that Hell sensed the Elomic energy that emanated from one angel in particular: an aura that showed brighter than the rest. So, the great lumbering mountain turned to digest this angel. With eyes that covered her body, she saw through multiple pupils this angel's battle against others of its kind. Broad shouldered, muscular, and wielding a sword that was imbued with power from fire itself, she became more aware with each digestion of an angel.

The ingestion of these creature's life experiences merged with her own. Experiences that she could use to increase the suffering of those trapped alive within her gullet: suffering that elongated would cause those trapped within to live forever as she regurgitated their life force to them in a give and take of life. But this angel she now hunted was stronger than most; his light shone brighter, drawing her. She accessed the memories of those that floated within her fiery gelatinous organs and a name floated into her consciousness.

Michael.

Closer she inched herself towards the angel. And what level of vision she possessed could see the blurry image in the distance of the uniquely bright biped that moved. It was quick, and its hacking movements caused other lights to be repelled back violently or fall to the earth. And she noted their lights grew dark and cold. She would have this life. For another predator that terminated Elomic life, she could not stand. Only one could feast in the school of angels that flew around her, for with two legs this creature above all others emanated the glowing light and life of the Creator that could sustain her.

"Sheol." he had called her. "Thou art the answer that must be raised in the future. My response to those who say the ways of the Lord are not equal. For with thee will I give reply and say, 'Have I not allowed thee to depart and live thy life apart from me? To live thy desires to thine own hurt?' Yea Sheol. Sleep until my vengeance is awakened. Sleep now."

And so, the lumbering angst of God did so; deep in the rapid eye movements that only a living mountain could dream. Rumblings of lava and ancient fire quieted until the anger of the Lord would rupture to be revealed later in Creation.

But now she had awakened from her slumber, and now… the great mountain hungered. Her rousing had brought sustenance to her. Like fireflies, she saw the wondrous lights that flickered against her skin; lights that moved with faces and with each consumption; her awareness was made keener in the realization that she consumed entities that possessed the life of the Creator. Creatures who, through the draining of their life's memories, she learned called themselves Elohim, and the one who created her: God or El. They had named her Hell. And with each light she consumed, she found the light strengthened her, made her wiser, and brought her senses into focus. Each light was different in taste and texture. Some were of the same house she had learned. And for reasons she was piecing together, all seemed to be presently in conflict with each other. All divided into factions, and two names rose above all others to the surface of her consciousness: Lucifer and Michael.

Thus, deep under Heaven, Hell grew. Nurtured by forces now arrayed against her and she sensed a strange fire, a wavelength of energy that she had not seen since her awakening. And as a moth attracted to a flame, she turned towards it. Her path now emptied her into the channel of carved rock created by passing temporal storms. Storms that jettisoned away from the center of Limbo to find their home in the great cyclonic winds that were the Abyss. Hell lumbered as she roasted alive angels that were foolish enough to impede her and careless enough to bar her path.

She crawled, stretching her protozoan-like body, then pulling the same: her amoeba-like movement clawing her to a place where she would savor this newfound source of food. Thus, like all that travel the path of Limbo, she made her way to the heart of the domain. The center of the Realm of Choices: The Nexus.

The Prime Realm: The Ancient Past

Argoth had seen enough.

He had allowed himself to be captured and bound and had feigned helplessness. But he was Grigori, and he would never allow himself to be so helpless as to have no recourse.

He noted that many of his guards were watching the developing storm that grew. And he did what was necessary to free himself from his captives.

"Run!" he screamed.

The Grigori had already stood on his feet and lifted from the floor. The launch of a temporal storm from the gate was imminent. With his arms tied, he ran away from what he observed were the previous channels the storm had taken. The ground was clearly dredged from where previous storms had traveled to exit Limbo.

None of the guards gave chase, and Argoth noted that Michael and his men also moved swiftly to take shelter. He ducked into a crop of rock that faced away from the throne and crouched to become as small as possible.

His dagger materialized at will by his side, and he closed his eyes to concentrate. The blade upon command narrowed and its edge became increasingly thin, and he commanded the blade to insert itself between the ratchet of the shackle and paw of the device, and the blade slid as bidden and inserted itself as far as it would go. He then pressed his wrists against a rock to tighten the cuff and his shackle grew tighter but only for a moment as the shimming of his modified dagger worked and the cuff opened, and he slid his hand from his restraint. He repeated the process using his free hand and shook the manacles from his wrist and they fell to the ground.

    He peaked over the rocky barrier he hid behind, and the throne was barely visible and awash in light. He was sure others saw what he saw; that a temporal storm was about to erupt from its womb. Air visibly moved towards the swirling portal, and he could feel his own breath leaving his lungs. Energy coalesced into a swirling ball of prismatic light. He gasped for air as the portal inhaled the breath of life from all things that were in proximity to its reach. Rocks and all things unsecured to the earth floor flew into the giant portal and Argoth suddenly felt heavy as the weight of his own body seemed to force him into the ground. The phenomenon was increasing the gravity in its presence and fissures materialized in the ground as particulates of dirt increased in their own weight. The sound of crashing rock and rushing wind surrounded all things, and he struggled to keep upright when suddenly there was quiet, and the pressure subsided. Argoth knew that this was the moment experienced by all things living; that Limbo itself now transitioned from inhaling to exhaling: and instinctively, the angel ducked.

An explosion as the sound of crashing waves echoed throughout the chamber. The portal then collapsed on itself and erupted in color and wind; as all things that had been sucked into the portal previously were now jettisoned as deadly projectiles towards anything that was in their path. Rocks and dust shot from the gate and dust itself was as sandpaper that would shear boulders to pebbles and strip all exposed flesh. Boulders exploded and Argoth turned his face away and misted as the boulder in front of him disintegrated from the blasting winds. He quickly floated to a deeper ditch within which to hide and he peeked to see an orb of temporal energy that was where the portal was previously. An orb that raced and scooped up matter only to fling it into atoms before peculiarly reassembling it again into some disfigured former copy of itself.

It was coming.

The scourge of Limbo and the scourer of the corridors thereof, of which all living things fled. The temporal storm was here, and it jettisoned in screaming fury from the portal from which it was birthed. Its course was set and Argoth knew that if he stayed where he hid, he should be safe. But he watched as some angels failed to understand that one could not stand in the storm's path; angels who failed to comprehend that eternity was simply a component of time itself, and a component time had the power to dismantle. And for those of the Mists that failed to move quickly, they too were sucked into the grasping winds of the storm. And Argoth watched as two angels did not move quickly enough nor hid themselves deep enough. And as dust, was removed from their hiding places and pulled into the wailing gusts of the storm. Argoth watched as their molecular structure was disassembled. He watched as blood vessels and their heart stones and wings de-constructed into the base elements of existence: elements that now floated as particulates enlarging the rotating winds that was the temporal storm.

The tempest moved closer and Argoth now ducked his head and tightened his body as much as possible into a fetal position. The storm marched over him, and the gales shrieked its presence. It wailed like Eladrin, the King of the Ophanim, and even misted, Argoth could feel the tug of the storm despite his attempt to escape its grasp; for though phased from angelic touch: time itself reached out to seize the cohesive elements that made up the angel's celestial body. And Argoth could feel the storm reach with its tendrils into his very cells; could feel the separation that was beginning even as he helplessly hid as much as possible from the storm that raged above. Pain wracked through his person, and he strained with all of his might to become smaller and distant from the outlying reach of the temporal winds. To do anything and all things necessary to escape from the storm's reach. But his body was also subject to the tearing of matter that the storm's grasp exerted on all things it touched. And

Argoth screamed out in howling agony. For he could feel that he was being ripped open alive: stretched as if upon a torturous medieval rack. And his screams lifted into the chorus of the howling winds that emanated from the moving storm. And in the moments that the storm moved overhead was an eternity for the eternal living angel. And Argoth lifted his hand before his face and the limbs disassembled before his eyes. It phased in and out of existence, as angelic veins and subcutaneous tissue became exposed, then phased into nothing… until it did not.

The pain suddenly stopped, and he looked overhead and the storm had passed over. His body relaxed, and he felt that his form was as it should be. The angel was sore, and his muscles fatigued as they fought to keep his flesh connected to his frame… connected to his skeleton, even as the bones and marrow of his body had begun to de-construct. Argoth sighed and lowered his head in relief.

A sigh from knowing that one had survived a brush with death. And although dissolution was not something that naturally would occur to an Elohim. He knew that there existed heavenly forces within Creation that could threaten even his existence; and on this day… he had encountered such a force.

He stood to his feet to see what remained of friend and foe. He saw Raphael and quickly rushed to his side. The angel had also wisely hidden in a deep pit in the ground and had covered himself with rock.

"Are you alright my Prince?"

"I am fine. What of our peers? Can you see them?"

Argoth looked to his left and to his right, and the haze from the storm's passing settled, and he could see Michael and Ares kneeling at a rock.

He pointed for Raphael to see. "What are they doing?"

Raphael narrowed his eyes and his vision cleared and he sighed, "Mourning."

Argoth moved slightly to his side to see that embedded within the rock and within the floor were limbs and faces of the angels who had made up Michael's party. And where there had been a group of angelic bounty hunters commissioned to capture Lucifer and his allies, now there were but two; two angels who now cried in anguish: wailing over the spectacle of fused dead angelic bodies that lay spread about in their path.

Argoth's ears turned up and a humming sound filled the room.

Ares and Michael also took note that something was amiss.

"Another storm?" asked Ares.

"No," said Michael. "Something else."

The air around the Nexus suddenly changed, and a breeze fluttered through the chamber. Dark clouds churned circularly. Emerald and sapphire lights flickered as a portal opened behind the remaining four angelic brothers. The air sizzled and smoke recoiled to reveal a man who walked through the portal. His eyes were aglow in blue light, and he stood draped in all white with a bow across his back and a purple sash was draped over his chest, and when he had completely stepped through the spatial gate, the portal closed behind him.

He eyed the group that slowly stood to their feet to face him. Each face that beheld his own was dirty with cuts and draped with blood. He saw the fused bodies of hands, faces and wings in the floor and he smiled and spoke.

"I am Leto Alexander. I have come for the throne and the power of this realm. I have come to extinguish life. Be not afraid. You believe in God, believe also in me."

Raphael spoke for them all. "We accept no God other than El."

Leto replied, "Pity… then come and learn why I am called… the Beast."

The Prime Realm: The Ancient Past

Jerahmeel could hear the cries of his brothers behind him. Through translucent sheets of ice, he could make out the distorted images of Michael, Gabriel, and Talus' muscular frame. Although, they were but a haze behind the ice; their presence gave him hope, hope that though he may fall. Heaven would be buttressed by his brethren behind him. Hope that there would yet be a standard to protect the people of the land.

He raised his axe. Its blade was chilled and instantly froze all matter upon which it touched. White smoke lifted from its edge like steam as if the weapon breathed.

He lowered his axe, and upon it lowering, a creature of the mist froze and shattered.

Cries and ghostly screams erupted into the air, and with each swing Jerahmeel grew tired.

Jerahmeel's breath betrayed him, and his lungs took in great gulps of air to saturate themselves once more. His muscles were sore, and he had no way of knowing how long he had been fighting. He just knew that his back was to a wall of his own making and before him was a door that shimmered blue and released ghostly entities that spoke incessantly over and over but one refrain.

"Feed the Mists."

Jerahmeel saw that more of the floating creatures poured from the portal that was the Gate of Limbo. He eyed them as they drifted as fog above the floor and watched as smoky human and arachnoid-like figures rose from the creeping gloom. And though many were slow; their movement replicated the plodding nature of smoke itself.

Perhaps, he thought.

He eyed the portal the more, and then felt the thick wall of ice he had created behind him. His touch confirmed his worst fears. The ice was melting literally from his own exertion and the external temperature of Heaven's basement and the heat of battle.

His brow furrowed, and he gritted his teeth. He steeled himself for the struggle that was forthcoming and determined that his position could not be held.

He must go through.

Jerahmeel inhaled and then exhaled and lifted his axe to cut down by frost the forming enemies set before him. As a plow, Jerahmeel trenched through his foes, scattering them to the left and to the right. Enemies disintegrated as shards of ice and puffs of snow before him. Closer he approached the shimmering blue gate that was the Gate of Limbo. Its waves of energy could be felt now. It expelled radiation that blurred the air and caused the same to move. It spewed phantasmal energies that radiated from the Nexus: energies that warped time and space and which were held together by the very word of God.

Another foe was dispatched.

He turned his head to hear the faintest of cries.

"Jerahmeel!"

The muffled call of Michael and his brethren reached his ears. He took a moment to catch his breath before the next wave of creatures came and turned to see the opaque figures of his brothers beating against the thick sheet of ice he had erected. He watched their anxious shadows pace back and forth and the pounding that shook the wall he had made. And noted small cracks form from his brethren's efforts to breach his barrier. He could, of course, add more layers of ice and stall their inevitable entry to assist him. The angel lowered his head; for he could also heed the tempting call to bring down the thick sheeted wall of ice he had barricaded himself within; and he contemplated the dangers of venturing alone into the Realm of Choices: a decision wrought with risk. But he was one, one who would sacrifice himself, if need be, while his brothers could secure this position together better than he could alone.

He once more sighed, and then turned his back to his brethren and his face to the sapphire gate before him. And with axe in hand, he determined to bring the battle to the home of the mists themselves.

And with gritted teeth, Jerahmeel entered the Gate of Limbo. The azure entrance embraced him into its welcoming arms, and the angel disappeared in a flash of cobalt light.

The Prime Realm: The Ancient Past

Leto Alexander warped through space and time and stepped from the portal of his making unto the dank soft earth that was the floor of Limbo. A pungent smell akin to rotting leaves and decayed flesh assaulted his sense of smell, and he turned up his nose. Blueish and white light emanated from before him, and giant obsidian pillars towered to his left and right. Each was etched with glyphs and the whole of the floor was illuminated, and a great bluish gate swirled in front of him. And set in its center was a black onyx edged seat that looked to be a throne. Four angels also stood before him. Two knelt beside a body of a third that was smelted into the earth. Whilst two hovered before him and turned to face him. Their faces were covered in purple hoods, hiding naught but glowing eyes. And scattered as a path to the steps of the throne were bodies of creatures and angels that were melded into the gravel-like ground.

Leto smiled knowingly that he had arrived at his desired destination and spoke to the assembled group before him.

"I am Leto Alexander. I have come for the Throne and the

power of this realm. I have come to extinguish life. Be not afraid. You believe in God, believe also in me."

Raphael spoke for them all. "We accept no God other than El."

Leto replied, "Pity… then come and learn why I am called… the Beast."

Michael and Ares stood to their feet and withdrew their swords. The sounds of metal sliding against metal rose into the air, and Michael opened his mouth to speak. "I deny your claim to the power of this realm. Return thou from whence thou came. Or dissolution will be your end."

Ares whispered to Michael. "Why does he look like Lucifer?"

Michael shook his head while shrugging his shoulders lightly. His eyes locked on his adversary's movement.

Leto reached behind his back and removed his bow and knocked it. He pulled the string back and replied. "Here is my answer."

Leto released the arrow, and it whizzed through the air as it zeroed in on Michael's chest. Michael watched amused as the bolt traveled towards him, then turned to his side and he caught the arrow. He then threw the dart back at its sender and the arrow flew and penetrated Leto's shoulder and he screamed out in agony.

"I told you, human. Your claim is denied. How a Clayborn has arrived to walk the shores of Limbo is a curious thing indeed, but you will depart, or your next injury will see thee headless."

Leto squirmed as he removed the arrow from his shoulder and threw it to the ground. He smiled. "Very well then… I accept your challenge." He then walked towards them all. And with each step he took, his wound healed.

Raphael's dagger materialized to his side and both he and Argoth mutually released their blades to accost the approaching human. Each zoomed towards Leto's face to impale the human, but when they were within arm's length, both blades fell out the air and dropped to the ground.

Leto's eyebrow raised, and he chuckled as he continued his march towards the two Grigori. Argoth took up a defensive position in front of Raphael and misted and flew to enter the human and partially rematerialize with intent to render him harmless. But as he flew closer to the man's presence, he felt virtue leave his body, and he too fell from the air and landed on his feet. Leto walked closer to the angel, who choked as if gasping for air. And as Leto walked closer to Argoth, the angel felt weaker still and vomited.

Leto simply stood next to the angel and looked down at him. "Foolish child. You do not yet understand who and whose I am. Only now, toward the end, do you comprehend. But I will not take your life… not yet." Leto then looked upon Raphael. Raphael moved to back away from the human. Leto grinned and nodded his head. "I see you are wiser than your fellow here. You understand… good." He then walked unobstructed towards the path that would cause him to walk directly into Michael and Ares' path.

Both angels raised their swords, and Ares was first to launch into attack. His speed was that of an Elohim and in his assumption, he overestimated both his speed and strength. And he brought his blade to slice the throat of Leto. But Leto was not human. He was Nephilim and his speed and strength matched that of Ares to the angel's surprise and he moved as quickly as Ares such that the angel's attacks missed. Each weaved and dodged until the weaponless Leto landed an open palm to the chest of Ares and sent the angel reeling back into Michael's waiting arms. Ares lifted himself from Michael's grasp and spoke. "There is power somehow draining from me. I can feel my life leave my body… and flow into him. He can somehow siphon life from us. How, I do not know. But his touch accelerates the phenomena. I am considerably weaker now. He cannot be allowed to touch us. Nor do I know the distance within which he may be attacked."

Michael nodded and looked at Raphael in understanding as to why he kept back from the fray. He then looked at Leto, who had stopped momentarily to allow the reality of the angel's circumstance to seep in.

"So," said Michael. "You are the fabled Nephilim I have both seen in my vision and was spoken of by Lilith from the other realm. You are the Abomination, a hybrid of human and Elohim. An anathema of Creation and the purposes of God."

Leto smirked. "Perhaps what you say is true angel… perhaps. But Creation need not worry itself with my existence but of her own, as once I have returned her back upon itself, all will be well. For I know the ways of El and know that though he is able. He will use his agents to do his bidding. But tell me creature, what agent present can hope to stand against me… you?"

Michael stood indomitable with sword drawn, and upon mental command caused the blade to split as a fan extended, and seven swords unfurled themselves out as a peacock's spread tail.

"An impressive display angel." said the Antichrist. "An impressive display indeed. But one that will not avail you." Leto then proceeded his march towards the Chief Prince, weaponless and defiant in his gait.

Michael's eyes narrowed and three swords upon his command launched themselves towards the human to cleave the man. Closer they crossed the distance between the two combatants and when the blades were within arm's reach. Leto weaved and eluded the first sword, and then, with a twist of his arm, caught the second blade by the hilt and with it deflected the incoming third sword that now circled him and joined the first in their dual attempts to stab his person.

Leto, imbued with angelic strength, overpowered the swords' mental command from Michael to leave his hand. Leto crossed swords as the two swords, still under Michael's control, hovered in the air, countering his movements. Leto smiled and spoke aloud for Michael to hear. "I am disappointed. Is that all angel?"

Michael frowned and released three more swords to accost the hybrid that men would one day call the Beast. Each flew to join the two blades already in a twirling dance to pierce the acrobatic Leto. The hybrid of creation who moved unlike a human but that of an angel. Leto bowed and rotated his torso, and with his open hand, caught another sword. And now, armed with two of the six blades that accosted him, Leto fought off the other four as if he fought four men.

Ares raised his voice. "How can this thing be that he can handle the instruments of angels?"

Michael looked on in shock and awe, unable to answer his fellow as Leto, though struggling, continued his steady advance towards him.

Raphael, looking upon the spectacle, raised his voice. "Hear me legions of Limbo. For I stand as the eyes of God and speak with the voice of Lotan. Come to my aid, shades of twilight and feed. For this one here has virtue to spare. Come... and feed the Mists!"

Immediately, eyes pierced the darkness, and the hissing sounds of creatures that moved in the black could be heard. Low growls, scratching and rumblings echoed off the ears as shadows elongated, then retreated beyond the sight of all present.

"Call them Grigori." Leto huffed. "I do not fear them." He then smiled, turned and jolted into the adjacent black and into the multitude of yellow eyes and snarls.

Michael's swords trailed after him and when the barrier to the shadow was breached, he lifted his hand to recall his swords and the blades withdrew from the dark and upon them was green blood that dripped from the edges and several creatures akin to centipedes fell off the flying swords and to the ground unmoving and sliced in half. The swords returned to their master's hand and merged into the prime blade: all save two.

And the angels looked into the black and saw stroboscopic flashes that revealed the image of a man with two swords. And in front of him and to his rear were spider-like creatures and bi-pedal forms that accosted him from all sides. But the man stayed upon his feet, and with each flash the eyes saw heaps of creatures dead at his feet, and eventually the growls of the dark were silenced. And the flashes stopped.

Then the dark itself seemed to move, and a figure strode from the darkness into the light and behind him trailed two swords that scraped the surface of the ground and sparks flickered into the air as the figure slowly revealed itself to be Leto Alexander. And he grinned as he walked towards the quad of angels that stood as a blockade before him.

"Fear, emissaries of your god. For I have come that ye might have death. And have it more abundantly."

Michael lifted his sword and pointed towards the Nephilim and roared as he launched himself forward to engage this threat to existence and Ares, Raphael and Argoth joined with their peer to engage the Beast as one man.

* * *

Lucifer Chi watched the behemoth that was Hell plod along its path. It's behavior no longer focused on the legion that attacked it, but on… something else. And the Chief Prince noted that as long as they did not attack it, it did not respond in kind.

Gadreel, a commander of the Host, also noted. "My Lord!"

"I see it," said Lucifer. "It appears to no longer seem interested in us." Lucifer then surveyed those that were once arrayed against him. "Nor the Grigori, it seems."

"Your orders, my prince?" said Gadreel.

Lucifer's eyes narrowed, and he contemplated his next action. "We cannot destroy the creature. Cease our attack."

Gadreel then took a trumpet from his side and gave three short blasts. Immediately, those under the command of Lucifer broke off their attack.

"The Grigori still accost the creature, my Lord."

This too, Lucifer noted, and lifted himself into the air at Gadreel's words. He extended his wings and the pipes within his arms and throat could be seen, and the prince of angels belted out his words for all to hear.

"I decree a truce, House Grigori! Parlay with the chief prince and let us tend to a greater threat to us all. Come and let us reason together!"

Immediately, a Grigori materialized in front of Lucifer.

"Speak," said Lucifer. "So, you were near me this whole time. And close enough to smite me down?"

"We were always nigh thee, Chief Prince, even in thy mouth. What words would you have me record that would now proceed out of thy mouth?"

Lucifer nodded, "Very well then. We must unite forces. For neither thee as a house nor I and our might absent the Grigori can with these numbers fell the beast of Hell. Are we agreed?"

"The thing is, as you say. But for what cause would you rally us? Hast, thou changed the reason for which we have left the capital of Heaven to seek solace amidst the shades? Do you repent of thine actions to compel House Grigori to heel?"

"No," replied Lucifer. "I do not repent of my actions. But repentance is not required for our union at this time. There are larger issues at play than the squabbles that plague our people. What in existence could cause the creature to leave us and turn to parts unknown? Surely you see that the thing is primordial. It hungers and our kind engines its appetite. What then would cause it to turn away from us?"

The Grigori's eyes narrowed. "You think it has found a source of nourishment other than our order?"

Lucifer turned to look into the distance as the creature continued its slow crawl towards a distant light. "I do not profess to know this thing, but it clearly travels to a source, nonetheless. A source of power that would have it turn from a host of God's angels. And I am forced to ask, what could cause any in creation to find our attention lacking? What power could draw the attention of a consumer of angelic flesh that the beast would turn? To what attracts it, I do not know. But it is a power that has drawn the eye of the greatest thing to manifest power in heaven save El. Let us go and see for ourselves this power and see if it is a threat to Heaven or no."

The Grigori's eyes narrowed, and it turned from Lucifer and

looked out into the cavern at its brethren. And thousands of now visible eyes also narrowed, and all turned to the one before Lucifer and it too turned towards the Chief Prince and replied. "We are of one mind in this thing. Lead on."

Lucifer nodded and he turned to his lieutenants. "Where is Michael?"

An angel replied, "He was last seen…" and the angel pointed in the direction that Hell traveled.

"Are you sure?"

The angel nodded.

"Then it would seem that my brother is ahead of us in this knowledge. Give directive to the commanders to close ranks and to follow. The rest of you are on me… forward!"

And the assembled host of Heaven followed Lucifer Draco as he led them all to follow the path of Hell. A path that led them all to the center of Limbo… the Nexus.

* * *

Michael of the Chi Realm flew as fast as he could, and he approached the light that drew all the life of Limbo towards it. Like a moth to a flame, he too was attracted to the pull of the scintillating center of Limbo. He drew closer and could make out dark shimmering globules that hung in the air from black tendril like stands. The pulsating orbs seemed alive, as if something within constrained to be released. And as he drew closer, it shone brighter and projected images on its skin.

The glow showed Lucifer, and he was haggard, and dirt covered his face. But he stood upon his legs as if wobbly and he raged aloud to the God of Heaven and saw two creatures Michael had not seen. And Lucifer changed his form and floated towards them. The thing was curious to Michael, and he drew closer to see other floating orbs light up as he neared their presence. For in one Heaven was engulfed in flames and Michael watched as El had touched his forehead and saw images of El upon hewn beams of wood and his hands were pierced and Michael was struck for the Eternal one was dead! Flustered by what he saw, he continued to move towards the light as more globules came into view and others seemed to drop to accost him with their images. For some showed black tendrils wrap themselves like pythons and enshroud many in heaven and Michael saw they were cast out by the anger of the Lord as lightning to the four corners of existence. Yet, other images showed Lucifer with a sword drawn attacking the Lord and nick the heel of God to bleed.

Images of brother fighting against brother flooded his eyes. And the angel struggled to remain on his feet, and he wavered to hold himself steady. Vertigo overcame him, and when he looked up, another orb lowered to his sight and within it was… himself. The mirror image stood strong within the Kiln, and he held a sword that fanned out into seven blades, each that circled the angel in an orbit as electrons circle a nucleus. Flames engulfed the chamber, and a figure walked with a familiar gait towards Michael in the orb. Despite the fury of fire, there was music that accompanied the walk. The darkness peeled back against the flickering flames to reveal a face. The face of familiarity and of brotherly love. A face that revealed the melodic grin of Lucifer.

"Nooooo!!!" Michael cried. "Why, Lucifer, why?" Michael slammed his fists into the ground.

Michael turned his head to the right to see another orb drop from the ceiling. Its image was unmistakable. For within the orb was a mountain of living fire. A living, craggy organism that belched fire and brimstone. A roar emanated from the globule. The familiar sound of the creature Hell that was behind him. But this roar was like a more developed creature. One that was far more massive than what the Host in Limbo now fought against. Michael trembled at the sound, and he watched as the image showed an angel swallowed alive into the belly of the beast. It spewed fire and brimstone and its roar shook the streets of heaven.

It was in that moment that Michael knew the fullness of his brother's capability. His predilection to lead the whole of Heaven to destruction and yeah even bring injury to El. It was at this moment that Michael's heart changed towards his brother as he fought to move past the orbs that attempted to show him the future. It was then that Michael could make out the shapes and visage of several angels that seemed to be engaged with a creature unlike any he had seen before. And Michael looked at an angel who was identical to himself. An angel who commanded multiple swords and whose movements mimicked his own. Closer he approached the light that emanated from the Nexus and beheld Raphael, but not Raphael, Ares, but not Ares and Argoth, but not the Argoth he knew. But it was the final face that gave him pause, the image of himself that fought along the three, and all were in combat, seeking to bring down what seemed to be a creature whose form was like their own. And Michael remembered the words used in one of the visions to describe the creature before him that his angelic duplicate fought: human. But a human masked with the face of familiarity: Lucifer.

* * *

Azure lights flashed around the head of house Harrada. Jerahmeel's walking through the door into Limbo was to greet a tunnel of stars that elongated and contracted as he stepped forward while streaks of prismatic light whizzed past him. Unknown voices whispered about him as he walked, and figures of his past, present and some he knew could only be from his future paraded themselves in and out of his field of vision and hearing.

A singular source of light rushed forward to greet him.

Yet something invisible pulled at him, seeking to keep him from completing the journey into the land of choices. A gripping force... nay hands... invisible hands... choking him.

Jerahmeel's eyes bulged, and his lungs and his throat expressed their asphyxiated displeasure. But Jerahmeel would not be denied and stretched his hands outward, clawing at the air and pressing his legs against gravitational forces seeking to overwhelm him.

"AAAARRRGHHHH!" the angel cried. And with a last lunge forward, Jerahmeel pierced the barrier of irradiating light and he broke through its illuminating veil as a moth from a cocoon.

Jerahmeel stood hunched over in darkness and he turned his head behind him to see a wall of light receding into the distance until it became naught but a pinprick, and as it fled, he could hear whispers in the dark that faded with its retreat: whispers that mouthed the words, "Feed the Mists."

He allowed himself to catch his breath and to survey his surroundings. He had never entered Limbo; even when it served as the causeway bridge between the kingdoms of the Seraphim and Elohim. The work of the capital and its governance never allowed such fancy as to see the fabled home of the city of fire: Ashe.

He had heard stories from Raphael and others of the beauty that was Limbo; an in-between kingdom: a realm of light and wonder. But this place was dark, cold, and dank. Towering columns ancient in design stood as cathedral-like sentries in hallways to parts unknown. The floor was cracked and in many places, giant boulders floated and shimmering lights twinkled on the floors and ceiling, as if phasing in and out of existence. Great hollowed caves exhaled gusts of wind and Jerahmeel walked towards a wall and placed his hand to feel its texture and it rose and fell.

"It lives?" he whispered to himself.

He prepared to lift himself into the air when he felt the rise and fall of the wall and a strange mist was excreted from a small hole within its stony skin. He shook his head and waved his hand to clear the foul odor that now floated in the air and when he did; he heard voices as if someone exerted themselves in battle; suddenly a vision waded into his view. And he took a step back as he beheld the image of Raphael, Argoth, Michael and Ares and they fought a creature with two legs and whose stature was smaller than an angel and who wielded no sword, but a bow was upon his back. And the creature mouthed great things against the God of heaven and yea blasphemy and withheld the assault that the four angels instigated against him.

And in the vision, both Raphael and Argoth, who stood by

his side, spoke out, "Come over to the Tempest Throne and help us!" and then the vision became obscured as it lifted as a cloud and floated away.

Jerahmeel's eyes darted to and fro and he beheld neither exit nor a way to return to the basement door of Heaven. He frowned, knowing that he had entered a realm deemed off limits to angels and lest the Lord extended mercy, his trespass would see him stranded from home. So the prince of all Harrada contented himself that if by his actions he could stop the Mists from establishing a foothold at the underside of Heaven, he would be satisfied.

Jerahmeel removed his hand from the moist wall and peered into the twilight depths. A light showed in the distance and he set himself to venture towards it. Thus, with the purpose of heart, he traveled towards parts unknown to find the source of the vision to perhaps help his friends. A path that all that ventured into Limbo must at some point intersect: the Nexus.

* * *

Henel looked at the dark sky above him and it erupted in streaks of lightning that raced in crackling lines across the lid of limbo. And the reporter, having left the past, but unable to alter its outcome, became unsure of his whereabouts; as his continued movement made the thunder to churn louder. He looked to his left, and darkness and jagged streaks greeted his view. To his right, naught but twilight came into his field of vision, and to his rear, grayness and mist billowed, revealing nothing.

"Do not be afraid," said the familiar voice of Janus. "Move forward, for I have laid a path before thee. Do not stray from the path I have laid for thee, lest you venture into an eddy or current of time that would sweep you away, and you would be lost even to me. Are you clear in this purpose?"

Henel nodded. "I am clear. You want me to continue this dreaded walk into the dark."

Janus's two faces turned and smiled at the man. "The choice of which path you desire is ever before you, Henel, son of James. If you desire. I can recall you too Argoth." said the black face with white eyes. "Or… I can send you forward to apprehend that which you have been apprehended: to restore thy father." said the white face with black eyes. "The choice is yours, human," spoke both faces as one.

Henel sighed, "I will continue towards my father. I have read enough of the scriptures to know that I should press towards those things which are before me, and to forget those things that are behind me."

Janus nodded and both of his faces smiled. "Ah, a reference

from the Apostle Paul of Tarsus. He, too, followed the path that would lead him towards God. You are wise to do likewise. And be not afraid. For within the mind of all men lies a nexus. A point of decision where volition causes one's destiny to turn to the left or to the right. You now enter that Nexus Adamson. Even now, I sense your mind's grasp for direction. To know every detail of your journey. Yet your concern for direction is misplaced. You need but move forward to take you where you need to arrive. Walk forward and your path will be enlightened before thine eyes. Have more faith in he who set you on the path, than in your ability to see and to discern the path itself."

Henel looked about him and saw nothing and replied. "Riddles in the dark, and despite your words, I cannot see where I am going. How will I know when I have arrived?"

Silence echoed in reply.

Henel's face then steeled, and he took several steps forward. Moving, nay groping through the dark as he moved; and light flickered under his feet. And with each step, his path became illuminated, such that he saw a path for him to walk. When he moved to the right or took a step to the left. The path disappeared and a strong wind buffeted him. Voices barely perceptible whispered to goad him to leave the path he walked. But as long as he headed straight ahead, a path shown under his feet. With increasing confidence, he moved ever forward until the fog cleared and before him was a maze of chasms. But the path now forked into two paths. Each leading towards a differing collection of caves. He stood still for a moment and pondered his situation.

"Ah, so you stand between two opinions." said the disembodied voice of Janus.

"Why didn't you speak earlier?" replied Henel.

"Because, Adamson, you must unlearn what you have learned. For it is incumbent on you that in the depths of limbo, you walk by faith and not by sight. For the Lord himself is a lamp unto your feet and a light unto your path. Has this not been so?"

Henel conceded that the light underneath him had indeed guided him to where he stood now.

"And will I be guided to the choice I am to make now?" said Henel.

"The Lord is always nigh thee, even where Light may not exist. But behold. For the Lord hath set before us all, Life and Death. Therefore, choose Life that both thou and thy seed may live."

"But both paths look identical," said Henel.

"Indeed, often many choices appear as such. Thus, behold the choice given to thy father. To the left is the choice he could have taken: a choice that would have led him to know the true

God."

Henel frowned. "And the path to the right?"

"The path where you will instead find your father."

Henel was about to step to the path on the right when he paused and spoke aloud. "This is a path that will lead me away from God?"

The reply of silence and the winds of Limbo echoed in the ante-chamber.

"Will my feet then be lighted to show me the path I must take?"

"No. For all paths that lead away from God, arrive at a point of inevitability. If you walk this path, you may find your father. Or, you may not, and instead be lost in the eddies of Limbo; adrift, destined to wander for eternity and halt between two opinions: until the Lord God judges and settles the dispute for thee."

"For before you are the paths that your father has walked. It was a path of struggle and pain and now his path lies before you now. It is rare that a human is privy to see the inner workings of free will. To observe the silk-like strands that over time will harden as iron cable to span one's life. You, Henel James, now see the invisible."

Lightning flashed above Henel's head, and in the shadow of the clouds were angels locked in combat. Their swords clanked, and Henel strained to see that he was surrounded by an army of angels that were at war with one another. Angels who were locked into battle over the souls of men. Fighting with neither quarter given nor asked. But engaged in a battle to influence mortal men towards their agendas.

"Why was my father so important that angels would war over him?"

Janus replied, "His was one of influence. For your kind wrestle not against flesh and blood, but against principalities and powers. And Satan was the prince of the power of the air. Your father was once the Chief Editor of the Jerusalem Post. His decision to run or withhold stories could sway the minds of millions. This, Adamson, is a power that Lucifer would always take an interest in. Your father was torn over a story that if released would have ruined many a political career and have grave consequences for his family."

Janus materialized in front of Henel. "Hold human. You think that perhaps your actions could have been a superior outcome than the one El had ordained. That your will had it been imposed would be better than Gods?" Janus seemed to look away into the distance and nodded his head as if he had received instructions on high. "Witness the favor that El bestows upon you. Observe and see what in Limbo can only be shown. The alternative paths of life.

Behold and witness the outcome of your desire and not El's had your own purposes come to pass: be not faithless but believe."

Janus waved his hand, and a globule of light materialized in the air. It showed images of Henel's father; images of the story he had discovered. The recording he had heard in the car garage at the Jerusalem post. Henel watched as his dad went to the editor to pitch his story and then wrestled with his decision, only to change his mind and destroy all evidence he had of the story. Henel watched as his father became sullen and the world, over time, became like ash in his mouth. He watched as his father read the obituary of a man whom no one cared about. The last holdout of Leto Alexander's murder at his party. His father turned to alcohol in remorse over his actions. And while Henel's father was present, he was a source of abuse to both him and his mother. All because of the decision to abandon the truth that he knew. A truth that could have ached at him. Janus showed Henel the spirit that tormented his father in this alternative reality. Spirits of shame and worthlessness, spirits of regret and self-loathing. Daemons who haunted him at every turn and who convinced him his life was worthless. Daemons that cajoled him, and pressed him until their lies became his truth and their will his own. And Henel watched as his father, in a drunken rage, took a gun to the temple of his mother while she lay sleeping and pulled the trigger. He then watched his own father silently creep into his room, place his hand on his sleeping head and with the same gun that had obliterated his mother's life, watched in horror as his father took his own. Only to turn the weapon finally on himself; satisfying the will of Lucifer's minions and of the Anti-Christ himself. The murder-suicide of the family of Ezra James.

Thunder echoed over Henel and the reverberations of its bass rumbled around him and made him jump. Henel fell back on his hind in shock and tears welled up in his eyes. As he watched the images of his father's life distill into blackness, and Janus stood where the glowing orb once floated in place and he barked to the man. "Now go, and see to thy father, and free him from the chains Satan hast held him bound!"

Henel took a deep breath, nodded and with fear and trembling, slowly stepped forward to walk the path that delved deeper into the realm of madness that was his father's mind.

* * *

Lucifer of the Chi Realm and several of his squads followed him as he trailed after Hell. The beast was clearly attracted to something far in the distance.

"Lord Lucifer, Michael is not in the camp."

Lucifer stopped his flying to hear the report of his lieutenant.

"Explain yourself commander."

"You were commanded to see to the whereabouts of our brother. We have sent scouts through the Grigoric armies and none report his whereabouts. Did you not command him to seek the heads of the Grigori?"

"The thing is, as you say," said Lucifer. "And your search has shown him absent from our number?"

"Aye, my Lord."

Lucifer paused and returned his eyes to the beast that he followed. "Is it possible the creature consumed him?"

The commander shook his head. "We have speculated about this, my Lord, and have consulted with the Grigori. They indicate that Prince Michael's grigori still pens his tome, and thus they say that Michael still lives."

"And yet he lives in defiance of my orders. Do the grigori know if he was accosted away from us of his own will and the location of my brother?"

"Aye, my Lord."

"And?" said Lucifer. Irritated that he would have to further query his commander.

The commander then pointed in the distance to the pinprick of light that shown in the darkness that was Limbo's horizon.

Lucifer scowled, for the trajectory of Hell also traveled on that path. A path that would turn the creature away from satiating itself on Elomic life.

Perhaps the beast follows Michael? Lucifer pondered within himself.

"And did he go of his own accord?" The Chief Prince barked.

"Aye, my Prince," replied Gadreel

Lucifer released a heavy sigh and the sound of grumbling was heard in the ears of all. "Then he is absent without leave. Go to and muster the rest of the Host to follow me."

The commander nodded and saluted. "And what of you, my Prince, what shall you do?"

"I shall fly ahead of the beast and reach the point where my brother travels before this creature can. I will search for my brother and he shall be made to give an account of his stewardship. And perhaps I may also find a weapon to destroy this atrocity. For it cannot be allowed to breach the surface of Heaven. Are you clear in your purpose?"

"I am clear, my Prince."

Lucifer then spread his wings and lifted himself into the air and replied, "Then see to my orders and do not engage the beast lest attacked."

"As you command my prince." Gadreel watched as his master departed and flew off to overfly the crawling beast that was Hell.

* * *

Michael perched himself quietly behind and above the Temporal Gate. He eyed the goings on before him and his mind was challenged to grasp the totality of what he beheld. For before him, Raphael, Ares, Argoth and a duplicate of himself was fighting what looked to be a man. But this creature was unlike any he had ever seen. Now the Lord God had hinted that he would create a fourth race. And it was clear that Jerusalem's construction was to hold a population that was far larger than Heaven's own angelic population. Thus, Michael wondered within himself who this creature was. The battle that ensued below him showed that he somehow siphoned Elomic energy from those he fought. And he wondered within himself if this being was who Hell now crawled to claim. The being that could cause such a creature to ignore angelic armies.

"Why are you here?"

Michael did not look up, and merely replied to Lucifer's voice. "Do you not see what lies below us? Here is the center of Limbo. The locus from which the storms derive and the final destination for which Hell ignores us to come."

"You failed to obey my orders."

"Aye, brother… because you are not God. And despite what you might think. I am quite able to exercise my own volition.

Of course, it appears that we have a much larger issue to contend with. For is not Raphael dead? Yet I see him being accosted before my very eyes. And how is it that I see myself engaged to stop a force that seems to mimic the great beast in its ability to consume our kind? This brother is the battle we are meant to fight. Not the Grigori, because they choose to not obey you. Now still yourself from offense and see who… or what they fight. And tell me whose face do you see that could turn the creature of fire and brimstone. Behold the visage my brother, and explain to me why four of our brethren are now in arms?"

Lucifer stood mute, rebuked, and merely gazed at the combatants below him, bewildered. There were no words for him as the evidence before his eyes was unmistakable as he looked at the creature that the angels fought.

A creature that looked exactly like him.

* * *

Michael, Raphael, Ares, and Argoth panted as they stood to bar the Antichrist's path to the Tempest Throne. Each taking in breaths of air from the exertion to stop Leto Alexander's march towards them. All warily eyed him, while Leto looked past them all to gaze upon the chiseled obsidian rock that comprised the Tempest

Throne. He eyed the Elomic writing of God. Script carved by the Almighty's own finger upon the ancient pillars. An ancient language he had never seen, yet somehow could read and understand. For Leto possessed the knowledge passed to him from Janus, and was able to read the runes that were etched into the onyx towers and upon the seat of the Tempest Throne. Words hewn by the Almighty, written in his own tongue and with his own hand. And the runes, when translated, were written on this wise...

He who sits upon the throne of limbo, I give dominion to steward the Wilderness of sin and to subdue the land of choices, and lo, I set difference between the lands that are clean and unclean. And separate the lands of Heaven above from the earth and stars below. And from this nexus will the mouth of the Maelstrom be filled; until the time of Shiloh my scapegoat, who will offer his blood for the sins of the world. For I, the Lord God, hath declared it.

The son of Lucifer Draco then smiled upon his reading and looked at the array of those that stood between him and his prize and spoke.

"This power to bend possibility... to know all imaginable choices of the universe: no... the multi-verse. I will have this power. You cannot withstand me for eternity, as your very presence gives me strength. But I offer you once more the chance to bow down and to worship me. Do this and you also may share in my glory, but if not; know that I will cleave your bodies as a scythe reaps wheat. And your remains will be as chaff in my wake."

Michael stepped forward and stood before the rest of the angels that stood between Leto and the Tempest Throne, and replied for them all. "Do you think that we are slow to answer thee? But I say to thee nay. Get thee behind us Satan, for only the Lord God do we worship, and to him alone shall we bow."

Leto chuckled and shook his head in sorrow. "It is a pity that you cannot see the futility of your cause. Nor the foresight to see past what could be a new future for your people. But change is never easy. And I will force the children that you are into adulthood and bring to all realms freedom so that creation may exert her independence from God. I have seen the future. Have gazed into the eyes of even one of your own kind who has stopped at nothing to change his own course. I have deeded to that one a gift in the event that you do manage to stop my efforts. But I have prepared for such a thing. And though improbable it may be, your stand against me does nothing but awaken the very future you seek to avoid."

"And even in our pause, have you sought to study how I might be destroyed, not easily, I assure you. And know that I too have done the same and I conclude you are no threat to me. Thus, sadly, our skirmish will now come to an end." Leto then looked amusingly at Ares and said. "And to think that in a future age you will be called the God of War—pathetic."

Leto then smiled, and a portal opened behind him and he walked backward into the same and then disappeared into a cloud of blue and black smoke.

The cadre of angel's eyes widened and Michael spoke for them all. "Where has the devil gone?"

Raphael could hear the whine of turbulent winds behind them. A sound distinct from the swirling temporal gate that hovered to their rear. A sound he had heard moments before when Leto entered his portal, and a sound he now would associate with Leto's return.

A flash of blue light erupted behind them and the familiar black, churning smoke of a portal became clear as the entourage turned their heads.

Horror gripped them as the grin of Leto Alexander was spread wide across his face. For the Nephilim had portaled directly into the chair of the Tempest Throne and his hands gripped the onyx arms that protruded from it. He eyed them and he cocked his head to the side as he spoke to them all.

"You have failed angelic spawn and reality as you know it… is now mine."

Raphael screamed out. "No!!" And flew towards the throne, but Michael stretched forth his arm and stopped the Grigori and lifted into flight to descend upon his foe instead.

Leto smiled even the more and pounded his fist on the left arm of the Tempest Throne. The room responded in kind and the azure gate behind him sprung to life, and temporal currents and eddies erupted from the great ring in blinding blue light. Michael's ascent slowed as he succumbed to the temporal waves that now engulfed him. And time slowed from seconds into milliseconds and milliseconds themselves slowed to an infinitesimal crawl. Michael now hovered at the apex of his leap. His wings unfurled like a descending bird of prey, and the Sword of Ophanim was also unfolded into seven swords, and each was pointed in a downward strike to cleave the head of Leto.

Visible waves emanated from the throne and Raphael, Ares and Argoth found themselves also slowed. And having seen this portent in a vision, Raphael grabbed Argoth and shoved him aside so that they might escape the temporal cone of power that now flowed from the throne.

Michael meanwhile was helpless as he floated in the air motionless. Leto stood to his feet and lifted his hand to touch the cheek of his angelic adversary. "It is a shame that you did not accept my offer as now you have earned my judgment."

Leto then turned his back to Michael even as the angel continued to inch towards him and he resumed his sitting and placed his hands on the armrests of the throne.

"I redact you Michael, Prince of the Kortai."

And with those words, the great gate spun up in power and jettisoned a temporal storm from its loins. It spiraled in sapphire fury, and its circular form engulfed Michael in its grasp, and the angel screamed. The sound of his disintegration echoed in the ears of those present. His wail, the last thing to be heard before the atomic structures which kept his form together, dissolved and the temporal storm carried aloft the angel. His body reassembled and torn asunder, only to be refashioned again.

Raphael tackled Argoth and dove to the ground and misted to escape the storm's path. But Ares could not move in time and was caught in the trailing winds of the storm's rage and his body dematerialized and became one with the debris field that trailed it.

Argoth looked at the Nephilim whose power he had seen in a vision. A vision that saw the angelic-man rally the kingdoms of men to oppose God and his armies. A power that now sat upon the throne of possibilities, and Argoth, for a moment, would later journal that he experienced an emotional state uncommon to his kind: fear.

Leto then sat upon the seat of power and he rubbed his

hands across its stone arms. The gate of time churned above him and the mists themselves stayed within the shadows, unwilling to disturb the seeming new king that sat upon the Tempest Throne. Leto then spoke aloud blasphemy into the air.

"This throne is built upon the very stone that bedrocks Heaven, and upon this rock. I will quake the foundations of reality and turn back creation upon itself." The Antichrist then stood and raised his fist into the air and shook it defiantly into the azure-lit gloom.

"Behold Yeshua! A place mankind was never meant to see, and a place off limits, even to your angels. And yet I stand triumphant in one of your secret places, and see how your children cower before me: these living golems of flesh and bone. And now, by your own words and power, I possess the reigns of possibility and time itself. Now watch as I engine the destruction of all that you have made, and revert to nothing the work of your hands. By this throne, I will yield your own word to destroy this realm and all that it tethers. And your beloved scapegoat, your planned sacrificial lamb, will never have a wilderness to dispense the world's sin! And I, Leto Alexander, will do what my father could only dream. I will ascend above the stars, and will topple you upon your holy mountain. And I will be Alpha and Omega. And I will be God!"

A voice deep in bass and familiar in tenor clarioned across

the Nexus.

"You shall do no such thing, and it is clear that any creature that would name me as father has clearly lost sight of his station. For if a son honors his father and a servant his master: if then I be a father, where is my honor? And if I then a master, where then my fear?"

Leto turned to his rear and looked up to see that Lucifer and Michael stood atop the temporal gate, both with swords unsheathed and they looked down upon him, ready to oppose him, and he chuckled at the irony.

And Raphael and Argoth both smiled, relieved to see their extra-dimensional brethren.

* * *

Henel walked a path of darkness and as he took a step forward, a faint light goaded him to take another step further. The area gradually changed from dark and damp earth tones into a flurry of discombobulated images that were akin to movie screens attached to walls and ceilings. All were set within the midst of a room absent of activity save what appeared to be seven television monitors. Three monitors hung to the left of the bed, while three hung to the right. And one large screen stood above a man lying unconscious in a hospital bed. Various ones showed static on the screens while half showed the classic image of "please stand by." The center console was different and displayed an RGB-ribbon of colors. And in the center of the dark chamber the man in a hospital bed was connected to a six legged, heavy duty IV pole. A drip-line was connected to his arm and some medical type of machine made a small hum as it pumped the man with life-giving fluids. His eyes were closed and his breathing was regular, and Henel knew without a shadow of a doubt he had found his father and he draped himself over the sleeping man that sired him and wept.

Janus watched the man curiously and spoke. "Why do you weep, Adamson? You have found that which you have sought and have arrived closer to the task given thee by the King of Kings. Do not weep. Weep if the cause for which thou hast been apprehended fails."

Henel ignored the angel who had now revealed himself and, with head laid atop the chest of his father, he wiped his eyes and the sniffles lessened. The man then stood to his feet and spoke aloud to the angel that hovered inches from the ground. "When I left work yesterday, he was like this. It seems like I have been here for weeks. But I have been here only for a day. Is that correct?"

Janus nodded in affirmation.

"Then his condition has not changed from when I last saw him. If I am to lead him to Christ, how do I touch the consciousness of a man who is unconscious?"

Janus's two faces pursed their lips as one. "Aye, that would indeed seem impossible, but with God, all things are possible: behold."

And with those words, the first of three monitors to Henel's left ceased its static, and an image appeared in black and white on the screen. Images of children playing appeared on the monitor. Janus walked over to it and he turned his head slightly in curious observation. "Is this you Adamson?"

Henel also walked towards the screen and he looked at the image and it was of him and children from his primary school playing three-sticks in a schoolyard. Henel laughed as he remembered the memory. Three-sticks was a simple game, really. The goal was to jump between three sticks laid on the ground and then to spread them further and further apart. One could not touch the sticks, nor could a person step more than once in the spaces between the sticks. Henel watched as he failed in his last attempt by taking two spaces. The other competitors pointed and reacted with delight that he had lost. And reminding the young man that he could not jump such a distance. He chuckled as he watched the screen.

"Whose memory is this?" asked Janus.

Henel thought for a moment and then turned from the monitor to look at his father. "It would seem that it is his. Because, while I do remember this; this point of view shown on the monitor is not mine. As I think about it, as I was playing, I never even realized he was there. I just remember my dad picking me up from school right after this. But, I never knew he was there watching me play."

Henel turned back to the monitor to see that his father was smiling at his son's attempt to win. The enormous grin was indicative of a father's pride.

Another monitor then came into focus and shouting from its speakers roused Henel and Janus to turn their heads from the former screen. They now focused only their attention on the latest picture that was before them, and yet this new image was far less pleasant. It was an argument between Henel's mother and father, and it was laced with cursing, screaming, and the throwing of glass.

"You don't give a damn about this family. It's a story! It's a fucking story, Ezra!"

Ezra replied. "But it's not just a story. How am I to stand by and do nothing knowing what I know? I was never raised to turn my eyes from injustice. Am I supposed to start now? You knew what kind of man I was when you married me. If we let this evil persist, to grow and to go unanswered, do you think we will remain safe? Leto will find us, baby. If the Alexanders find out, we know what I know. They will hunt us and they will kill us. The only thing we can do is to use what we know to fight back, or better yet, bring the entire family down together."

Henel's mother frowned and picked up a picture of young Henel. It was a picture of his younger smiling self. A picture taken when he was in primary school and Henel remembered taking the portrait as he sat and fidgeted with his shirt and tie. The portrait was then shoved into the chest of his father and his mother pointed her finger at her son in the picture and replied. "Explain it to him. Explain it to Henel when he doesn't have a father. Oh, that's right. You'll be dead and will leave behind a son unprotected from the very thing you claim to protect him from. You can't protect him or be a father to him when you're dead, Ezra."

Henel's mother then stormed out of the room.

Ezra held the picture of his son and gazed into the photo and bit his lip as tears welled up in his eyes. He then spoke to the picture of young Henel. "Please forgive me, son. If you can ever find it in your heart please… please forgive me."

The screen then went static and Janus spoke to the staring and tear filled Henel James. "And have you done so, Son of James?"

Henel sniffled and then scrunched his face in confusion. "Have I done what?"

Janus's two faces stared down at the man, emotionless, and both his faces tilted in curiosity towards Henel. "And have you forgiven your father, Adamson?"

Henel paused in reply. He turned away from the monitor and stared at his unconscious father. He noted his pores, the color of his skin, and the way his hair partly covered his right eye. He eyed this man who walked away from him and his mother when he was young. A man he came to slowly understand. The sterile smell of hospital rooms permeated his nose, along with the lingering pungency of his father's body odor. A stink that hinted of the smell of age wafted into his nose, and it triggered Henel to think of the mortality of his father and his own. And Henel realized that while he lived by the will of Yeshua, who had made his home on earth. His father still fought the last enemy of mankind, which was death. And understanding that resolution was more important than retribution or restitution. Henel ushered the words to bring his release, and to release the consciousness of his father's torment over his decision: words he now ushered in prayer.

"Lord, I release the debt my father owes me. The debt a father owes to a son, and where my heart still calls out for repayment, when my own thoughts would seek to exact vengeance, please help me forgive, even as you have forgiven me for my own sins. Help me in this thing, God. Amen."

Janus nodded and replied, "El hast granted thy petition and now you are ready to see more, and after you have laid down thy stones. You will offer the gospel to thy father that he might be saved." Janus then extended his hand to Henel. Henel noted the gesture and placed his hands in the angels.

"Now take thy right hand and place it over his forehead and I will allow you to commune with thy father. But be careful, though I create the doorway, you must choose to enter. There can be no victory save the exit of you both. Fail and your mind will be lost in his. Your body will collapse before me and you shall be trapped here within the realm of possibility. Do not do this if you are not committed to the risk."

Henel looked down at his father and returned his gaze to the two faces of Janus. "And if I succeed, he will rise from his coma?"

"Perhaps, the thing is not mine to know. It is El's but if not, know that he will do more than be restored from a mere coma, Adamson: he will have eternal life," said Janus.

Henel looked back at his father and placed his hand on his father's forehead, inhaled deeply, and spoke. "Here I am Lord, send me."

* * *

There are few that understand the deep bowels of Limbo. Fewer still has seen her engorged with rage. For, far away from the pristine sky of Heaven and below the basement of the same; ancient angelic powers engaged one another in multiverse destroying combat; whilst legions marched behind the living embryo that was Hell. A creature borne out of time and which traveled towards the heart of Limbo itself: the Nexus. And while it neared its quarry; two brothers fought side by side against what angels would call Abomination. A hybrid creation that was half man and half angel, the pre-incarnate son of Lucifer, the Dragon and the being whom men would one day call: the Antichrist. Two brothers and two grigori attempting to stop a being who could usher the annihilation of all things.

Thus, Raphael watched as Lucifer, Michael, and Leto Alexander fought with one another. And he did the duty of his kind, which was to record the doings of all things.

Michael was the first to enter the fray and with sword in hand, he slashed at Leto, who side-stepped his swing and who used his bow to block his attack. Each turned, and Leto matched Michael's movements.

Leto lifted his bow and caught the Sword of Ophanim, preventing Michael from moving the weapon. Each strained against the other as their strength matched only by their wills to never surrender.

"Give up creature. Surrender now and perhaps there may even be mercy for thee. But continue in this… continue in this…" Michael then grabbed his chest and collapsed down to one knee.

Leto smiled as the effects of Michael being in such proximity to the Anti-Christ took its toll.

"What is happening to me?" Michael spoke aloud.

Leto smirked in satisfaction and walked closer to Michael, and with mental command, he summoned the Sword of Ophanim to him and the sword slowly left the hand of Michael. Startled, the angel struggled to grip the hilt and with a thought directed at the blade, to cease from its action to leave his hand, but it was too late. Leto had drained too much of the angel's life force into his own and the blade no longer saw Michael as its bearer, but he whose scent was of its master. And Leto raised his hand, and the sword flew into it.

Argoth, Raphael and even Lucifer were dismayed, and all knew that before them stood a being unlike any, they had previously encountered.

"Only now do you understand the nature of your failure. Only now has it sunk in the degree of my power. Before you, Chief Prince is not just a man, but also angel, and an angel with the power to siphon Elomic life. Thank you for your trinket. I have seen the future in which this same blade was forged to confront the mighty Lucifer. Let us see if the thing be true."

Leto then threw the blade towards Lucifer's direction and, upon command of Leto, it split into seven swords and the blades slashed at the Chief Prince of Angels.

Immediately, Lucifer hardened his skin and one blade skimmed off his armor and the High prince unsheathed his own sword and parried the blades that now accosted him. But Lucifer was the perfection of angels and he was the Light bringer; he who could move at the speed of light itself and his speed was such that the swords could not reach him and with his voice he vibrated the air and stilled one blade as the force of his words stopped the sword cold and it was caught suspended in the air. But the Chief Prince caught one blade between his palms before it could strike. He twisted his body and sent the sword back, flying towards the source of its control. Leto ducked to prevent his skewering.

Lucifer shouted. "Assist me Michael; although the creature is strong, he is not invincible!"

Michael slowly regained his strength and reached out with his mind to summon the sword. The blade paused its attack upon the Chief Prince and reassembled into one sword and returned to Michael's hand.

"See, he may indeed be able to siphon our power. But he cannot keep it; keep your distance if possible."

Leto smirked. "I suggest we test this claim, shall we?"

He then jumped towards Michael and, to the angel's surprise, punched him square in the jaw, sending the angel reeling into a column. Lucifer grabbed him from behind but Leto elbowed him in the abdomen and Lucifer immediately hunched over in pain. Leto then spun and, with a roundhouse kick and smashed the sole of his foot into the face of the Chief Angel, sending him headfirst into the dirt.

Leto reached for Lucifer, thinking he would grapple his neck and suffocate the angel. But Lucifer raised his hand and a flash of white light rose from his palm and blinded the man.

Leto staggered back and screamed in anguish. "My eyes! My eyes!"

Lucifer rose to his feet and wiped blood from his lip as he watched Leto place his palms over his face to both shield and sooth his eyes.

Leto then froze and smiled. "I can feel you Father. You are too close, and now you are too late."

He then armored himself as do the angels of Heaven, and he leaped unto Lucifer and Lucifer turned his head but his turn was too late for several of his teeth were jostled loosed by the hammering blow of Leto into his father's jaw, forcing the mighty angel to his knees. Blood trickled from Lucifer's lip and he spit a tooth from his mouth.

Lucifer slid his wrist over his lip to wipe the blood from his mouth and his eyes narrowed, and he brightened as a star such that Michael and those in the vicinity had to turn their face to keep from blindness.

"You dare strike the Chief Prince? Do you know who I am! I will rend you from end to end and your entrails will serve as reminders to those in your future that the past has said, we will defy you, and to come no further!"

Lucifer then hovered over the Nephilim and grabbed him by the throat and Leto coughed out his reply.

"Aye, father. I dare. And I dare to not just strike at you but all of creation before I am done."

"Insolent whelp!" Lucifer roared, and he pummeled the man such that even the bruises on his face bruised, but Leto took the beating. Allowed the wrath of the father to be administered unto him. For though he was Nephilim, the creature had a grigori who was missioned to never interfere. And in the course of transcription he noted for the annals of Grigoric history that the man allowed himself to suffer at the hands of his father. For Leto had seen through the eyes of the Sephiroth the possibilities of his future. He had tasted the future and knew that soon the sound he waited for would rescue him and launch his plan into action.

And the man was not denied.

A roar then echoed across the chamber. A guttural sound that was at once animalistic, primal and menacing. And the giant beast Hell raised herself upon legs of magma and opened her mouth to unleash the announcement of her presence, and her mouth was full of fires and lava such that if one peered into the monstrosity that was the living mountain; great worms floated as schools of fish within her innards and her breath blackened the air and the smell of sulfur smacked at the noses of all.

Leto saw Lucifer turn his head at the beast's arrival and, seeing he was distracted, took an arrow from his side and plunged the tip into the right eye of Lucifer, who unleashed a cry of pain and staggered back in anguish.

Leto then raised himself and scampered away from the angel and rushed to grip the arm of the Tempest Throne. And upon his touch, the great seat sprang to life and the obsidian columns that draped its sides lit up in blue light. Great arcing tendrils of alternating current snaked up and down the onyx spires as the hum of the gate of limbo awakened and the circular portal behind roared to life.

And Leto looked out at the throng now arrayed against him. For Hell stood before him and to its rear was an army of angels who marched and flew in formation behind the beast. Thousands upon thousands ready to do the bidding of Lucifer, and a million spears who upon command would unleash the torrent of their military might upon the Anti-Christ who sat upon the Tempest Throne.

Leto then readied his defense and issued the mental command to the gate of Limbo. The command to unleash a Temporal Storm and obliterate them all.

* * *

The amoeba like form of Hell slithered into the Nexus. It surveyed with its reddish eyes and saw its prey standing within reach of digestion. Angels of such power that they could turn the head of the behemoth and ignore the legions that accosted it: only to taste the unique flesh that was before it.

For, nestled within the heart of Limbo, were two princes with direct connection to the Creator's presence and a creature whose aura was also unique: an aura unfamiliar to the creature Hell. For it was an aura that was of the Elohim race but was not. A being that carried the image of God, yet somehow was laced with angelic blood. And Hell pondered this alternative source of food. A source she had determined she would savor. And when Hell saw the three engaged in battle, she paused to see this display of angelic power. For even in her primordial state, she was a creature that would hunt its prey when it was most unaware. To position herself slowly, to creep ever closer inch by inch until her arms were within reach to snatch her bounty in her pyroclastic hands and her digestive tape worms could do the work of consuming her meal.

Thus, Hell saw the power of Leto. A power to siphon Elomic life and to take it as one's own. And in her watching, she beheld a competitor for the nourishment that flowed through the heart of every celestial being. And in this thing, Hell would have no equal. No rival that would vie to take from her what vengeance demanded. And so the beast turned her head towards the Nephilim and engaged the Antichrist. And with her entry into the battle, she would contend to be the apex predator.

Her roar carried across the ceiling of the lower depths of Heaven, such that even above, the ground of Heaven shook. Like a volcano that spoke; her voice shattered rock, and ancient columns obliterated at her cry.

Her rocky tendrils flung flowery flaming rock-like eyes towards the Abomination. And as pyroclastic flow that fell from the sky; two fell to surround Leto and from the pyres, isopod-like worms emerged as pill bugs; unfurled and treaded towards the man. Carrion, similar to the creatures that lurked within the mists. Carrion that would leech the power of Leto Alexander and absorb him into the lava-like mass that was Hell. For in all the realms, Hell would not be denied her sustenance. Her instinct for survival was fueled by the vengeance of God, and in the end, there could be only one.

Leto turned to face this new menace and his eyes widened, stemming from a cocktail of surprise, and ice cubed with fear. But like his father; pride swelled within him as well, and despite this challenge, he would not be denied. So the Nephilim reached into his quiver and launched arrow after arrow at the crawling worms that scurried towards him. And though many of the bolts found their mark and staked the millipede-like beasts into the ground. Hell was a massive, mountainous-like amoeba. And though individual isopods could be destroyed, the creature herself could not be denied. Her relentless hunger would be satiated and this Leto instinctively knew for he recalled from the memories of Lotan that in his future she would be a beast whose fires could not be quenched and her worms died not.

He spun the oncoming beast and settled into the Tempest Throne. And with his mind and will, activated the great azure gate that hovered overhead. And upon the mental command, the wellspring of time's fury spun to life, and temporal energies swirled in circular fashion.

"I will not be upended by you, beast. I have seen a future in which I have sparred with you and lost. But I am now ready and armed to contend with you. For in your coming to find me; your seeking has cost you your own doom."

And with those words, the gate crackled in blinding light

and from its eye a temporal storm was ejected and jettisoned towards the path of Hell.

A spherical twirling ball of white light, bathed in arcs of lightning, raced from above Leto and over the throne. The tornadic roar bellowed the Tempest Thrones fury. Its sound, engined by ancient winds, engulfed all ears as it passed and thousands of angels instinctively ducked for cover as the weaponized sphere of time orbited across the cadmium ceiling of Limbo's throne hall. Columns carved by the touch of previous storms had formed a tunnel and cathedral-like chute that stood like an honor guard as the temporal storm passed overhead.

Plasma arcs reached out in all directions and individual angels found themselves caught in the voltaic arms of time only to be disintegrated and then reconstructed again: but to be newly assembled into grotesque forms that were partially phased into rock and stone. Others lost their appearance of youth, only to be recreated as walking skeletons that collapsed into dust under their own weight. And while some escaped the storm's touch: all were shaken to their core.

The temporal orb was unstoppable. A catapulted payload of time now shot to detonate directly into the incoming monster that was Hell. And the vengeance of God moved undeterred at the sight; creeping snail-like, ever forward to engage Leto and the

Chief Princes.

The Host that flanked the beast of Hell moved aside, knowing that they witnessed an immovable object preparing to confront an irresistible force. And the whole of Limbus watched as the temporal storm smashed into the rocky and lava-like skin of Hell.

The beast roared as the temporal storm saturated the creature. Light and lava exploded with one another as volcanic lightning intertwined with the elongated arms of temporal strikes and their union forked across the ceiling of the realm.

Alabaster blanketed atop whiteness and the chamber and angels covered their eyes and winced and turned away from the sight. But when the light subsided enough to peer into the happenings of when eternity meets vengeance, it was clear to all standing that eternity reigned victor; for the temporal storm had passed through Hell and had continued its unbending march. And Argoth noted that the worms of hell which did not die, were indeed not dead, but had been transformed and now bore the likeness of fine strands of twine and were a far cry from the fiery and parasitic helminths they had been, and Hell herself was as a stump or mound of mud and bubbled like the hot pits of Earth release methane gas. But the fearful beast that devoured angels and which drained the Elomic life of the same was no more. And the great temporal storm spiraled down the long throat of Limbo to be deposited into the

Maelstrom. Unabated, unstoppable, it roared in thunderous fury as it spiraled away.

Argoth watched as some angels dared reach out to touch the remains of Hell, and when they did so, their hands burned and they withdrew them yelping from the searing pain only to find that their hands were now withered and lame. And when the dust had settled, Leto Alexander stood triumphant in front of the Tempest Throne and surveyed the decimation of Heaven's forces. He watched as angels were snuffed from existence and he grinned in satisfaction, knowing he witnessed the destruction of his foes and spoke aloud his pleasure.

"See Yeshua! See how easily I have extinguished the vengeance of God and have denied you and the Father the pleasure of my incarceration. Behold, oh Ancient One…," Leto said smugly, "and see how easily I turn the Trinity's power upon its own head!"

Leto then turned his face towards his father Lucifer who, like all his kind, had sought retreat from the temporal storm's reach. And Leto eyed the angel and spoke aloud his insolence. "Know that you are a failure… a blip upon the tapestry of creation and your sole success lies in your conception of me to complete the one task you could not: the downfall of creation and of its Creator."

And Leto stared down upon the decimation and smiled knowing that victory was now at hand.

Act III

The Journey of Henel James

Henel touched the forehead of his father, as instructed by Janus. He closed his eyes, and he felt himself leave his body. Floating... falling... drifting upon currents of thought, emotion and regret.

"Will thyself Adamson. Find the core of your father's angst. It will be a black stain upon his soul. Find it, and when you do, tell me what you see."

Henel strained his eyes to see past the flood of thoughts and flurry of emotions that surrounded him as he moved between the ether of his father's mind. His path took him between twisting globules of memory-flooded light as he drifted past the dreams and unrealized visions of his father. Henel searched for the void Janus spoke of; searched until he saw a swirling blackness. It was a circular orb similar to the images he had seen from telescopes or computer models that had captured the shape of black holes. A darkness surrounded by light. An onyx accretion disc that sucked into it all hopes, fears... and faith.

"I see it," said Janus. "It appears to be drawing all things within it."

"You see that which every man carries if not filled with the spirit of God, Adamson. A void that will feed upon all things internal to your soul. Until there is nothing left. This Adamson is the sin nature. A consuming lust, it is. A gravity well full of the pride of life, the lust of the flesh and the lust of the eyes. It is a thing interwoven into your nature such that without Yeshua, it cannot be removed. It is the thing that cannot please God, an abyss of sorts. And one that cannot simply be dislodged from your mortal frame. Therefore, a new body your kind must possess. For the sin nature is an all-consuming thing. Taking from your bodies even the breath of life once given to thy kind by El to Adam. A degenerating influence that breeds sickness, disease, and mental anguish your kind was never meant to experience."

Henel looked at the black swirling void and replied. "What do I do?"

"Enter the dark," said Janus. "Enter the dark place that is your father's mind and soul, and within, you shall at last find your father."

Henel balked. "You want me to go in there?"

"I want you to save your father. Go, or leave him forever to the black, but the choice is yours."

Henel frowned. For the sight of sin resident in the body: to see the sin nature like this was a terrifying thing to see. It was a corrosive black that seemed to feed on the very life that was his father.

"Sin is a parasite." He said aloud.

"Indeed," said Janus.

"And am I then the exterminator?"

"No," came the angel's reply. "Only Christ can terminate sin. You are simply the vessel he uses to bring his blood and love to eradicate the stain of sin. Do you understand?"

"Yes," replied Henel. He then moved and floated towards the orbiting darkness within his father's mind... to enter the depth of sin.

Closer he floated towards the black orb, and as he grew nearer, he could feel the tug of the sin and the weight of his form begin to move faster towards the orb of swirling blackness. Like his earlier experience in the ladder, he felt himself become heavier. As if the weights of his father was now being placed upon him. And he suddenly collapsed into sorrow. "Janus!" he cried out.

"Do not attempt to take on the responsibilities of your father. Nor think you can carry such a load of sin. Only Christ can do such a thing. See them, but let the weights pass over you as water from a shower. The weights of your father are not your burdens to bear."

Henel concentrated and then let go. Realizing that the memories of his father, his anxieties and cares were not his to endure. That no man, not even his father, could carry such a load. As he floated towards the darkness, it was here in the depths of a comatose mind that he realized that the nature of man was not designed to carry such burdens. For man was made to depend on God. This disconnection is what exposed mankind to endure what was unendurable. But Henel was in Christ. He had given his life to Yeshua many years ago now. And he affirmed his dependence aloud even as he descended deeper into the black, and he pronounced his faith aloud. "I can do all things through Christ who strengthens me."

Henel noted Janus was correct. The weights did indeed lift as water leaves the skin after a shower. But his sensation of falling did not. And light and memories of his father now cascaded over him as he experienced the sensation of sliding down a chute. A panorama of images and sounds raced past him; memories and fractured dreams sprinted over and under him. And in the distance, Henel could see a tunnel of black illuminated by a pinprick of light that raced to meet him.

A speck of light that suddenly he was face to face with, but its appearance merely the opening to another "room". Henel stumbled in and, seated hunched over, was his father in a white hospital gown, wailing with his face in his palms.

And sensing that he was no longer alone with his thoughts. His father, eyes red and with an unkempt beard, looked up in disbelief and spoke.

"Henel?"

* * *

"See Yeshua! See how easily I have extinguished the vengeance of God and have denied you and the Father the pleasure of my incarceration. Behold, oh Ancient One…," Leto said smugly. "And see how easily I turn the Trinity's power upon its own head!"

Leto then turned his face towards his father Lucifer who, like all his kind, had sought a retreat from the temporal storm's reach. And Leto eyed the angel and spoke aloud his insolence. "Know that you are a failure… a blip upon the tapestry of creation and your sole success lies in your conception of me to complete the one task you could not: the downfall of creation and of its Creator."

Angels nearby turned and stared at Lucifer in confusion. Gadreel came to him and whispered. "Chief Prince… what is he talking about?"

Lucifer scowled, for the secret things of his heart had been revealed before all and in front of him stood an abomination that called him 'father'. And Lucifer could not imagine in what universe he would succumb to create this angelic and human hybrid that spouted such obscenities.

Lucifer then replied to the inquiry made of him. "I do not know. But knowledge is not needed. What is required for the present is action. And this creature cannot be allowed to upend us; nay he cannot be allowed to roll back Creation. We are the Elohim and will not allow it! I command all that are able to attack and to do so now and assist in this Abomination's demise!" He then waved his sword forward towards Leto and lifted himself to resume his attack.

But when Lucifer looked behind him to see who rallied by his side. The Host was a shell of what had entered Limbo. Even the ethereal grigori were on the ground and many had been affected by the storm's effects and were uncontrollably shifting between phases of intangibility and tangibility.

"Lucifer, we cannot fight this being and the power of the seat he commands," said Ares.

Michael then spoke and pointed for all to see. "Look, the storm returns!"

All eyes then turned to see what they believed to be the return of the temporal storm. But the crackling of plasma did not originate from the cyclone but from another power… another source. All backed away and formed ranks with spears at the ready to repel what was developing to be an azure gate that formed in front of them. Its coils of light reached out like lightning and caused sparks to fly as the bolts streaked against the cavern's ceiling and floor. Small fires erupted and a shimmering globule formed and then retracted, making the wind rush to fill the void of air behind it. And when the dust cleared, naught was left but three Grigori. Lilith stood to the left while Lotan was to the right and each held aloft Janus, who struggled to stand.

      Lotan then removed his hand from Janus' shoulders and raised his arms and a staff appeared. And atop its tip was a sapphire that was surrounded with an onyx diadem. And the Grigori slammed the base of the staff into the ground and a flash of light raced out in all directions and expanded in concentric circles. The expanding wall of light sprinted in all directions and illuminated Limbus for everyone to see. And the light revealed that to the sides of the Host and to their rear and fore were creatures that slithered, and ghostly apparitions with fanged teeth. All hissed and seethed with piercing eyes, ready to devour them all. For nowhere were the creatures not seen and even the ceiling was draped with octopi like beasts whose mouths were in their stomachs and they stretched their wings as hanging bats. And Michael made ready pikemen on all sides of their forces, for they were surrounded even from above from the hissing creatures.

      And the moving wall of white gained the notice of Leto and the light shown in the darkness; and the darkness comprehended it not. The illuminating wave covered the Tempest Throne and the Gate of Limbo that was behind the ancient seat of power. And Leto moved to sit within the throne and he once more summoned a storm from the recesses of the gate. Its power expelled a spinning ball of temporal power and sent the orb flying towards what remained of the host. But instead of moving with the speed of light, it instead moved at a snail's pace, and its speed, though tempered, did not negate its power to destroy, and with tendrils that obliterated all that it touched; the storm left from above Leto and the Tempest Throne to travel towards the arrayed Host.

And when the Chief Prince and all assembled saw they were to be accosted by another temporal cloud, but that it slowed such that it could be evaded; it was clear to all present that Lotan was the cause, and all turned to see the power that he wielded to have such an impact, and Lucifer remarked. "You are Lotan. El hast spoken of you Keeper of the Tempest Throne… what have you done?"

Lotan replied as he struggled with his raised staff to hold back the might of eternity itself and replied, "Given us time, but just an abeyance from the storm that the Abomination has unleashed. Now hurry, for we three can forestall the storm but we cannot stop its march. Hurry to do all that you can to get your people to safety."

Lucifer replied. "This thing we cannot do. We cannot allow the Abomination to remain seated on this throne of power. El's will be done, but we cannot abide this threat whilst we draw breath. He must be unseated."

Lotan then spoke to Janus. "Janus to me. I need your will to buttress the staff's power. Join me… hurry and grab hold; for eternity and I fight with one another. I cannot hope to be victorious alone. But the storm is not the only threat that we face, for the Mists themselves must be defended against, and only a Sephiroth can influence them."

Lilith replied, "Can the staff's power hold both the storm and the Mists at bay?"

Janus straightened himself and reached out to grab the hilt of the staff, along with Lotan, and replied. "We shall soon see." Janus then closed his eyes, and a pulse raced from his hand into the staff and shot out in a spherical exploding ball of light. The area illuminated from twilight to what was like the dawning of day. And the Mists moved back for the light shown in the darkness and the darkness comprehended it not. And for the moment relief settled over the assembled host, for the Mists were held at bay and the Temporal Storm seemed to also be held in abeyance. And some of the Host cheered, for never in their time in Limbo had they seen any force able to withstand a storm from the Tempest Throne, and cries rang out in adulation, "Hail Lotan! Hail Janus for time itself has halted her march!"

And the thing was heard by Lucifer, and he was displeased.

And seeing that the storm was held in stasis but not neutralized, nor danger from the Mists themselves removed. He moved next to Lotan and Janus and, in his pride, also placed his hand to touch the staff of the Grigori, thinking to add his own power to their own. For his thoughts were revealed when he handled the staff and were recorded on this wise. If they, being Grigori, could, with their power, hold eternity at bay, how much more should the chief prince be able to move the storm itself?

And when Lucifer's hands touched the staff, Lotan cried out, "No!"

But it was too late, for the staff released a cry as a woman in travail as Lucifer's power flowed through the weapon, and the energies were as strange fire and immediately the bubble of power that surrounded the host collapsed and a concussive force emanated from the staff. And Lucifer, Lotan and Janus were were knocked backward and fell onto their hinds as the eyes in the darkness brightened and the hiss and sounds of creatures scurrying in the dark echoed across the cavern.

Michael turned to his left and right, but the darkness was thick and he could not get his bearings from which direction an attack would come. "In El's name… they are everywhere."

Lotan lifted up his head to see his staff broken in the distance and angrily turned to the chief prince and said. "Why could you not abide in thy calling wherewith you were called? Is not the office of Chief Prince enough? Must you be Sephiroth too? Are you greater than God to know who should yield power? Alas, your pride and thine actions have doomed us all."

Janus replied, "What is done is now done, form ranks! They are coming!"

And as those words were spoken, angels on the periphery and those closest to the Mists found themselves under attack and some were dragged kicking and screaming into the darkness.

Lucifer yelled, "Michael, above you!"

Michael looked up and from the darkness, a bat-like creature descended with claws drawn to lift him away. But the angel rose to meet the beast and, with sword in hand, lifted his weapon to pierce its breast and upon mental command, the blade came aflame. And the beast was engulfed in fire and Michael pulled his sword from the creature's breast and it fell from the sky.

"Ares and Gadreel. Take to the air and prevent our being accosted from above. The rest form up on the Chief Prince. We must find a lateral path through the monsters."

"But my prince," said Ares. "We cannot fight these Mists."

"Perhaps not," yelled Michael. "But we definitely cannot stop the march of the temporal storm that comes for us all. We have no choice. We must escape the channel of the storm's path and into the darkness we must go."

Michael turned to see that the storm was indeed awakening to continue its march towards them. The effects of Lotan and Janus's magic were wearing off. So Michael ordered the Host to form a phalanx straight into what he believed was the west flank of the Mists, hoping to give space between themselves and the oncoming storm.

And the Mists hissed in the darkness at the light of angels that now began to penetrate their ranks, and the light of God's brave angels shown in darkness; and the darkness comprehended it not.

* * *

Jerahmeel could 'feel' the dark drape around him like a dank humidity that shrouded his skin. Voices within the black whispered to him, beckoning him to submit to the enticement to be enveloped… to be consumed. And yet despite the allure; the subtle temptation to surrender to fatigue and to close his eyes. The very desire had to be sublimated. Resisted. And just when the desire to rest… to sleep would surely overwhelm him, a wave of light illuminated the cavern. And the incessant child-like voices that surrounded him and that attempted in soothing pentameter to draw him towards them—screamed. The howls were the shrieks of frustration and rage, of goals deferred and of eluded prey.

And with the rising of the brightness; Jerahmeel could see the assembled host in the distance. And the army was surrounded by a moving cloud of darkness containing hissing and fanged creatures that both whispered and slithered in the dark. And to the fore of the army were two grigori holding a staff that pulsated and projected waves of light: a cascading power that seemed to keep the darkness at bay. And beyond them was a colossal and circular globe of lightning that crept towards them. The great storm cloud was a luminous orb that discharged strokes of lightning. An aerial phenomenon that was held suspended aloft in the air by a staff that two angels raised in defiance to the enormity that gyrated before them. White bolts of plasma ejected from its body and obliterated all that was touched. And Jerahmeel, seeing the host in such dire straits, quickened his pace and his wings beat with an acceleration that shot the angel towards the fray like a falling star.

But even as he approached; darkness enveloped the host and also sought to wash over him like storm surge. A blackness that provided cover for the things that lived within. And the angel looked and all he saw was the thousands of luminous angels which emanated with the light of God, and he beheld in horror as one by one… the lights began to go out like stars snuffed from existence by the grip of a black hole.

Jerahmeel watched as his destination of twinkling light slowly faded. But there was one light that pulsated stronger than the others. A familiar oscillation that was known to him… yeah, known to all: Lucifer. And Lucifer's light shone brightly to serve as a beacon to all as the Host moved into the darkness.

"Hang on, my brethren. I am coming." He muttered to himself.

But even as the words were uttered aloud, a doppelgänger of himself suddenly appeared to oppose him. And it barred his path. Jerahmeel attempted to go around it and the angel found that whatever way he moved, it mimicked his movement such that Jerahmeel could not pass to join his brethren. The creature smiled at Jerahmeel's efforts to pass him and spoke aloud to him.

"You have entered Limbus Harrada. And it is a domain you may not leave."

Jerahmeel's eyes narrowed, and his face grew firm. "You may possess the similitude of my appearance, but it is clear you do not possess my mind. For if Heaven can be saved, I do not intend to leave. But I intend to go through you." And the angel moved forward with his axe raised and brought it down upon the shadowy figure. But the weapon merely passed through ether and the dissipated fog of its wake then re-solidified to mirror the prince of

Harrada and spoke aloud. "Amusing… my turn."

Jerahmeel braced himself for attack, and the cloud image of himself formed an axe from the dust of the ground. The shade of Jerahmeel brought the weapon down upon the angel, seeking to cleave him in two. But Jerahmeel, seeing his own movement used against him, raised his hand and summoned his power to slow the motion of molecules. The creature's blow decelerated until it was naught but a frozen statue before the angel with its stationary axe raised high.

"You simply mimic me, but as suspected, you are merely a similitude of me. For I am forged by the God of the Universe and am justice personified. And I will not be stopped by a shade whose purpose defies the Lord's messenger."

Jerahmeel then took the hilt of his axe shaft, smote the frozen figure atop its head, and it shattered into pieces before his feet.

The angel then turned his head towards the fading light of his friend Lucifer and dashed himself towards what he knew could only be the attacked host. He summoned the god given power bequeathed to him by El, and the surrounding air chilled, such that a vaporous shield of absolute cold formed around his person.

He came to the edge of the host; and when he did, he saw below him shades fighting with his angelic brethren, and as he flew overhead, the ethereal creatures solidified to ice and shattered beneath him.

And Jerahmeel noted that Lucifer reached forth with his hands to touch a staff and the angel heard one of the staff's holders cry out "No!" And the rod released a cry as that of a woman in horrific travail and Jerahmeel saw that Lucifer's power flowed through the staff and the energies that manifested were as strange fire, and immediately the bubble of power that had surrounded the host collapsed. A flash of light ensued and Lucifer, Lotan and Janus were knocked backward and fell onto their hinds. The blast from the staff raced out in all directions and knocked Jerahmeel and many of the Host out of the air. The eyes in the darkness brightened and the hiss and sounds of creatures scurrying in the dark echoed across the cavern.

He lifted to the cavern sky once more and flew over the army until the distance between himself and Lucifer was crossed and he landed at the center of the host.

"Jerahmeel?" said Lucifer

"You seem to have a bit of a problem." And he extended his hand to his brother to lift him up.

Lucifer took Jerahmeel's hand and raised himself from the ground, "Your gift for understatement never ceases to amaze me."

Lotan then turned and spoke, "Brother, we could use your aid!"

Jerahmeel nodded and raised both his hands to the sky and the air around the edge of where the Host fought chilled such that any creature or angel that was caught in the barrier of cold Jerahmeel projected was burned from the frost of his power. The Mists moved back as some instantly became iced over and shattered under their own weight, while others were trampled over and crushed underfoot by their own kind as they retreated. Angels smote at those creatures not fast enough to escape from harm's way and the fractured crystal remains of teeth and creatures akin to snakes and arachnids fragmented onto the cavern floor.

Jerahmeel's power flowed through him and surrounded the army so that for a moment, the Host was safe. And the entire army moved under the cover of Jerahmeel's shield of cold and attempted to escape the clutches of Limbo to safety.

But the might of Jerahmeel to slow matter though powerful was not such that it could stop the temporal storm, and through the vapor and light, Jerahmeel could see a man atop a throne, and his eyes were as lightning, and the throne he stood in front of glowed with power and an azure gate swirled as if water rumbled within its eye. And it churned as if ready to spew death towards them.

But all took shelter underneath the canopy Jerahmeel had created, as they hurried with all speed to side step the massive storm ahead of them

* * *

"We cannot stop this storm," said Lilith! We cannot make it. There are too many of us and its reach will overshadow us."

Lotan and Janus replied as one man. "No. We cannot."

Lilith panicked as the winds of the storm made the ground to shake and the glowing orb of temporal power, though slowed, still moved towards them.

Lotan then touched Janus and spoke into his ear. "It cannot be done by us, for we are the keeper of the Throne. If it is to be done, it must be done by this one here. He who stands out of love to see to his friend and your Lord… Raphael."

Jerahmeel strained to keep his shield up. His brow was tight and sweat dripped from his exertion against the storm's power. And he was physically being pushed back. The ice shield began to manifest cracks, and as fast as Jerahmeel sealed them, more were created.

"The storm's power overwhelms me. Ugh… I cannot keep this pace up…"

Ice shards collapsed onto the host and collapsing glacier-like sheets of ice fell upon them and many scattered to avoid a frozen sky that literally fell upon them.

And fear came over the host. For the realization washed over them all that they had violated the command of God to not trespass into the Realm of Choices. The realization that the El had in his wisdom made the land off limits, and that because they had violated the Lord's command, they were now subject to the consequences of his wrath.

More shards fell, and several spoke aloud their angst. "We are doomed."

And to the front of the Host, they all could hear Leto laugh as he watched the storm he had unleashed obliterate his enemies before him.

And the storm's power cast its shadow and reached out with its disintegrating tentacles to overrun them all. Janus then touched Jerahmeel's shoulder and whispered into his ear and spoke unto him, saying, "This is the word of the Lord unto Jerahmeel, saying, Tis but a vapor of my breath, and who can withstand the blow thereof? Not by might, nor by power, but by my spirit, saith the Lord of hosts."

Jerahmeel nodded in understanding and spoke. "Thy will be done, oh Lord. Hear the cry of thy servant and save us God. Or we shall not be saved." He then stopped projecting the shield over the army and he ceased from his own works to allow the will of God to be done and when he lowered the shield, the storm overran them all. And its reach gripped to loose the atomic bonds that El willed to exist between protons, neutrons and electrons. And with the pulling apart of matter; light flashed before Jerahmeel's eyes and he felt the tearing asunder of his flesh.

And in that moment, when death towered over him. Jerahmeel stood defiant in the storm's path: defiant… and at peace.

His mind lost focus on all that surrounded him and his consciousness became attentive to naught but the presence of the Lord God Almighty. No Limbo, no Grigori, not even the disintegration of his own body. His mind uncluttered of all things save the awareness that he belonged to God, and in that instant; Jerahmeel understood what the rest of his brethren did not. That unless the Lord saved them, none would be saved. Lest the Lord build the house, all labored in vain to build it. That all of their efforts save those alone of El mattered. And with that knowledge Jerahmeel smiled, and the angel stood in faith upon the precipice of this revelation; and then knelt as the winds of time ripped his body and scattered his atoms to the winds. Knelt in surrender before the storm and did what none before had thought to do: to capture the power of limbo.

He prayed.

And Lotan and Janus recorded his words for all Grigoric history. Thus spake Jerahmeel, Lumazi and Head of House Harrada to the LORD on the day when the Antichrist sought to bring ruin to all of creation. And Janus recorded the words of Jerahmeel's disintegrating esophagus on this wise.

"I am the servant of the living God who is the maker of all, the Holy One, and the Ancient of Days. I do not fear dissolution for the Lord my God is with me. Though a thousand be slain before me, I will yet praise my God. Therefore, hear the cry of thy servant, oh Lord, and see this small one who stands before thy Holy Spirit and beckon to thy servants cry. For I am thy bondsman and stand before thy throne and command in thy name that this storm be stilled upon Limbus and let the will of thine adversaries be turned back upon their own heads." And Jerahmeel settled that though he might indeed see death, that even beyond his own existence, his prayer would live on in the ears of El and be answered.

And with the utterance of his words the remaining flesh of Jerahmeel was removed from his body and naught save a skeleton, muscle and several tendons could be seen as the angel was sandblasted alive yet yelped no cry for mercy, nor moved from his position of knelt prayer.

And in the sight of those that remained, the storm suddenly stayed, and the rotation of its howling winds stopped. And the Mists themselves were held in abeyance and their pillowed march was halted as the creeping fog was cut off as if by a wall of glass. And all eyes suddenly beheld the form of a man appear and stand over what was left of the knelt body of Jerahmeel. And the familiar voice of El could be heard from the swirling whirlwind and the image of Yeshua appeared as a cloud. And the Son of God spoke aloud and his voice made the ground to rumble. "Above all thy kind, only thou hast called for me. Now, be still and know that I am God."

And as quickly as he had appeared, the visage of Yeshua disappeared and Jerahmeel's form reconstituted and was made whole. And the angel inhaled gulps of air. The cyclone then turned as a hand turns a dial, and the typhoon of temporal power was released from its invisible grip, and it screamed in displeasure and was sent hurtling back towards the Tempest Throne.

Lightning strokes the size of skyscrapers lashed out to strike and disintegrate all objects within their reach. The Mists themselves joined in the storm's whine and the cadence of their combined shrieks were turned in anger towards Leto.

And Leto placed his hand on the throne to open again the Gate of Limbo and to summon a storm. But the Throne would not heed, for the King of Kings and he who sat upon the seat of the Universe had removed the authority to invoke his power. And Leto frantically slammed his fist down, thinking his blows would force the chair to obey him. And the light from Yeshua enveloped the storm as the Lord God returned the temporal torpedo to his adversary. For though eternity was primordial, Leto and all witnessed that in the beginning was the Word. And the word was with God. The same was in the beginning with God. And all things were made by him; and without him was not anything made that was made. And the power and light of God filled the realm of Limbo such that the light shown in the darkness; and the darkness comprehended it not.

And as the temporal typhoon churned towards the Antichrist; the Mists also now moved as an avalanche descends a mountain, and the scattering sounds of thousands of feet, and ghostly figures barely perceptible, could both be heard and seen. And they unleashed a collective wail that was as the sound of yearning laced with hunger. A mantra that was clear to all.

"Feed the Mists!"

Leto now stood, and he watched the wall-cloud of sin race as an oncoming tsunami to overtake him. Yet the Anti-Christ was smug in his belief he could weather this menace and he steeled himself and propped his chest out in defiance, thinking he could absorb the power of Elomic life.

And the army of ghosts swarmed and turned towards the head of the great storm. And like a fog that settles upon the valley. The mists deluged the cavern like a storm surge to overrun the throne and he who had sat smugly upon it.

And the wraiths shrouded over him and draped him in clouds of smoke that Leto's face could no more be seen. And he waved his hands frantically as if to clear debris from his eyes, and he turned to his left but could not escape the Mists. He then turned to his right and staggered as the living fog blanketed him to where the Nephilim panicked for the creatures entered his mouth and nostrils to choke the half-man half angel.

And Michael and those in his company beheld that Leto had the semblance of a mouth and the semblance of eyes where a face once was, and the abomination who had stood in defiance of God and his son Yeshua cried aloud with a blood gurgling, "Nooo!"

His choked screams filled the antechamber and his gasping voice rasped as he now thrashed on the stone floor accosted by the Mists. For enveloped by the wraiths of pride, he writhed as a trapped animal in the false belief that he could influence the dread fog. For they were not Elomic life but its opposite: Elomic death: the manifestations of sins whose forms were allowed to live and thrive in this secured realm until they could be released in an age yet to come. An age where they may one day reunite with their source and bring eternal repayment to the sentience that genesised their existence. Each creature now a gaseous manifestation of separation from God. An inevitable judgment that now consumed he who would one day bask in a lake of fire and brimstone and bathe in the second death. A locale the ghostly creatures would one day call… home.

The storm continued its climb towards the Tempest Throne, and the point of its origin. The crawling orb of tentacled lightning dragged along the floor and ceiling of the Nexus chamber. Its bluish light washed out all things in its glow and whatever was earlier disintegrated and destroyed was reassembled and made alive. And the roar of the storm was as the sound of howling winds that shrieked in competition with raging gails. And when the storm front reached the position where the Anti-Christ squirmed before the Tempest Throne the Abomination was swept away by the winds and the Mists that accosted him, and entered the azure gate that was the Nexus Gate of Limbo and vanished. The sound of a vacuum seal was heard and an explosive shock wave bellowed after from the circular gate and raced outward in all directions knocking all within vicinity to their backs while others were sent careening through the air. And the Nexus was lit in blinding light from the waves of energy that emanated from the gate. And when the brightness faded and dust had settled. Lucifer and all those within the chamber rose slowly to their feet to see that Jerahmeel now stood to the side of Lotan who was seated upon the Tempest Throne and to his right Janus hovered and his two faces looked out towards the throng of angels before them.

And as the multitudes looked at the sight, a large figure stepped through the gate and upon his head was a crown that said King of Kings and Lord of Lords. And above him was a figure like a dove, yet whose semblance was also one of an eagle. And five pulsating waves of energy blasted from the Azure gate. Waves that resonated against the chests of all present and in sync with five words that bellowed from the gate and all the floating globules that hovered within the Nexus.

"I AM, that I AM."

Immediately, all before the Tempest Throne fell on their faces, for the voice of El boomed and lightning and thunder ejected from the Gate of Limbo and before the Tempest Throne. And the voice of Almighty God reverberated in concussive force into the ears of all. And all floating orbs that hovered within the chamber also lit up in unison with El's voice.

"Have not I commanded that Limbo be sanctified from thy kind? Why then doth thou trespass upon the domain of my servant Lotan?"

Michael then stood up to address the father of creation and spoke, "I, Lord God, have done this thing, for it was to prevent bloodshed in Heaven."

The Holy Spirit then spoke, and his voice was the same

as El's. "Yet, hath not bloodshed already been spilled and yet you were not alone to compel the Host to defy my word."

Lucifer then looked down and rose from his prostrate position and lifted his voice to answer. "By my command was Heaven incited to leave and enter the realm of choices, my king. I and I alone have done this sin."

The Gate then turned black and the wings of the Holy Spirit were withdrawn and God's presence also withdrew where he could no longer be seen and all that remained was Lord Yeshua standing above and behind Lotan and those with him. And they were as ants at the Lord's feet. And the King of the Universe then spoke.

"Because thou hast done this thing, you and Michael shall remain in Limbo for a season to contend with thy choices, and with one another until thou would seek to no more wrestle to be first. For the last shall be first and the first must be last. For thou hast led a third of Heaven astray into the wilderness of sin and defy the command of God. For upon the day this lesson is learned thou shalt be welcomed home. And you house of Heaven have sought to war with thy brethren, now go to and return everyman to his house lest the ire of the Lord extend beyond the princes. For all have sought to do in the flesh what my servant Jerahmeel hast accomplished by my spirit. For it is not by power, nor by might shall the thing be done in my name. Now go and be about my Father's business."

And the Lord pointed towards the giant gate of Limbo for the Host to go through.

And everyman turned at the command of the Lord save Michael and Lucifer who stood behind and watched their countrymen walk past them and past Lotan and Jerahmeel and Janus.

And as each angel walked past the trio, they bowed their heads towards the appointed King of Limbo and saluted Jerahmeel. As they walked into the Gate and returned to their homes. And Raphael, seeing he too had entered Limbo and had sent his clans into the realm, also turned and he stared at Lucifer and Michael, who were silent and whose eyes were lowered to the ground. And he spoke to them and said, "God dealeth with you as with sons; for what son is he whom the father chasteneth not? But if ye be without chastisement, whereof all are partakers, then are ye bastards, and not sons. For verily for a few days shalt thou be chastised but for thy profit, that ye might be partakers of his holiness. Now no chastening for the present seemeth to be joyous, but grievous: nevertheless afterward it yieldeth the peaceable fruit of righteousness unto them which are exercised thereby. Do thy diligence to come quickly unto me, and I await your return."

Lucifer was silent and stoic, but Michael lifted his head, smiled, and nodded.

Raphael then inhaled and took Lilith by the arm and floated

towards the gate with the angel in tow and motioned for Argoth and Janus to follow, but the gate ceased to churn and turned white and the Lord looked upon his grigori and spoke.

"Hold thy peace. For with the four of you, I will have words. For I have much to say to thee and there is much to do that the contagion of sin might be reversed."

But to Lucifer and Michael, he directed also into the gate.

"You two go thy way, and when seventy years are completed in Limbo, I will come to you and fulfill my good promise to bring you back to this place."

And Michael and Lucifer bowed before the Lord and entered the gate and vanished.

And none but Raphael, Argoth, Lilith and Janus stayed before the Lord and departed not. The four grigori knelt, and the Lord revealed his will of what must now come.

* * *

Ezra James sobbed over the loss of his family. He knew he could never hope to see them again, and that their deaths, their targeting by the Italian Prime Minister Alexander and his son Leto, put them dead to rights into the crosshairs of assassination. Ezra had been warned via photos delivered to him anonymously. Photos that showed a man he had hired drop his wife and child off at Ben

Gurion Airport. Photos that showed them depart, and photos that showed them land and settle into their flat in New York City. Photos that assured him that despite all of his best efforts to sequester them to safety, they were not safe from the long arm of the Alexanders and that the family could and would extinguish them with impunity. He sobbed, knowing that his wife's death was on him. Sobbed because his pride cost him the love of his life and ruined a normal life for is son. And the man cried out in a guttural howl of grief and anguish.

"God, I have killed my family!"

Tears fell from his eyes and his jaw muscles hurt for his continued wails, but the flood of emotion would not stop: would not allow him release, and he choked on the guilt and regret of his decision to reveal what he knew about the Alexanders. "Oh God, what have I done?"

Occasionally he would look up to see them: images of his wife and son that assailed him. Ghostly apparitions that hovered over him as flies attracted to dung and that constantly asked him... why?

"What was so important that you would let her die? What cause rose to be more important than our own lives? Ezra. Didn't I warn you, Ezra? Didn't I try to talk you out of it? Didn't I tell you what would happen to us? But you did not heed the words of your wife. You never truly cared for us. You only just cared about that damn story!"

"That's not true!" replied Ezra to the black ghost-like figure that floated over his head. A figure that resembled his dead wife.

"I loved you... I loved Henel..."

"Then why am I dead?"

Ezra was silent in reply, and his head lowered into the palms of his hands and he wept. Wept until he could hear something join him in the imposed isolation he had erected for himself. And he lifted his eyes to see what or who would come to torture him. And his eyes widened in disbelief and sadness and he opened his mouth in conflicting emotions of confusion and expectation.

"Henel?" said Ezra. "First my wife and now my son comes to exacerbate my guilt. Go away, just please go away…" Ezra then motioned with a hand to shoo Henel away and to leave him in peace.

But Henel would not go and replied. "It's me, dad. I am here Abba, I am really here."

Ezra lifted his head to look at the person before him. He was not cloaked in black robes, nor his appearance changed with the shadow of turning. His image was static and in full color. And Ezra's eyes widened in cautious hope.

"Henel, is that really you?"

Henel nodded. "Yes, Abba, I am here, and you are alive, and I am alive. And I am here by your side."

Ezra's neck drew back in disbelief. "How is that possible? I know I am alive... I, I sense it. I also know that I am in some type of prison. I can't seem to get out. I've tried. You do not know how long I've tried. I see that door behind you, and I've tried to go into it. Hoping to get out of this room. But it shrinks every-time I go near it and moves away from me, staying just out of reach for me to exit, yet there it lies beckoning me to escape. But I know something is on the other side. I can sense that my freedom lies just beyond the door and that it is something that would let me out. But how did you get in?"

Henel replied, but his father cut him off. "Phfft, you are probably not even real. Like this one here. Probably another figment of my imagination. Leave me, boy, or whatever you claim to be. Leave me alone. You cannot be my son."

The black figure that looked like Henel's deceased mother hovered silently and hissed at him, and a voice echoed in his mind as the creature gritted its teeth and stared menacingly at him.

"Get out, boy. Leave now while you still can, and I will not have my fellows kill you. Nooo. wait... perhaps I will keep you locked here with your father and let your helplessness to save him eat at your soul and entertain me. You'd better get out, boy; get out while you still can."

Henel, having seen prominent men of God stand before evil, roused himself to courage and straightened his spine and stood defiantly before the creature. "Him I know. But you... I know you as well. You stink of rebellion, and reek of Lucifer, and in the name of Jesus. Leave him. You are not welcome here."

The figure seemed to struggle for a moment, then composed itself. "You are not the power here, boy. And as for me. I am not going anywhere. Not by the likes of you. I've been with him for a long time now. He belongs to me. And unless you depart. I will visit the sins of the father on the son. Leave while you still..."

"Shut the hell up," said Henel. "I said in the name of Jesus Christ of Nazareth, be silent."

Immediately, the creature could not speak. He struggled to mouth words; this Henel could tell. But it could not overcome the power of Christ. But something was not right... something was amiss. He should have been able to cast this spirit out. But yet it still remained.

The smoky daemon hovered over his father's head in pain and Ezra, too, winced in pain, but he noted the creature hovering over him and spoke up.

"Are you really here? I... I can just hear my own voice. Who are you?"

"I told you, dad. This is your son Henel, and I've come at the command of Yeshua… to deliver to you a message and if the Lord wills; to release you. And this thing here is besieging your mind and together… we will make it stop. I promise you."

Ezra stood up from his chair and looked at his son. He was much older than he remembered. But he could tell the recognizable features of his own and his beloved wife's face. Years could not erase the nose or the eyes. It was true. His son stood before him and Ezra raced towards him and hugged him. And Henel returned the gesture.

"It is good to see you, son," said his father.

"I missed you too, dad. I missed you, too. But we are not out of this yet."

Ezra released him and drew back slightly. "Please help me, son. Please help me."

"Abba, listen to me and listen carefully. God has not condemned you. Because before you ever thought yourself worthy of guilt; judgment had already been made in Heaven that all had sinned and fallen short of the expectations of God. There was no one… ever, who completely was right in his eyes: no one who fully followed Him. The entire world was condemned. Because when Adam fell, we all fell. We have taken on the same manner as our ancestors. To drift from his purpose for us, towards purposes of our own, in defiance of his will. You think you are a worse man because you attempted to expose another for his crimes? You think you are the only one who has suffered for doing what is right? No Abba, for there was none who could save us, save God himself. So eternity became clothed in mortality, and spirit became flesh to live among us and to pay the price of death none of us could pay and still, after the debt, be in relationship with God. So the Lord did the only thing he could do. He sacrificed his own son to pay the blood debt owed by us all. And in doing so released us to have fellowship with him and he with us. But to take advantage of this transaction, you yourself must determine that you even owe a debt that cannot be paid. That a creator exists to which you are accountable, and that you are guilty not of a crime to expose power. But of the crime of turning from your back from the love of God. You are guilty, Abba, but not for the crime, you think. You have failed to seriously consider that your life is not your own. Failed to acknowledge the one who has given you life. And now here in the dark recesses of your own mind he has come through me, to share with you the truth of Yeshua's redemption and to know if you will allow him to forgive you this debt and all those owed. Or will you opine here within your own mind, and continue to dole out payment on your terms for eternity? Will Yeshua be Lord? Or will Ezra James? You are the reporter and winner of the Pulitzer Prize in journalism. So I will ask you this last thing. Who is Yeshua to you, and whose will, will triumph today? You said you know that something lies behind the door that would grant you release. I will tell you what it is. It is HIM. HE stands at the door and knocks. If you believe in him, go and open the door and he will come in and you will sup with him and he with you. This is my promise Abba, and why I am here."

Ezra turned over the words spoken to him. They hit the deep places of his soul and he turned to see the hovering apparition that was silenced by any counter argument. He looked at his son, who seemed to possess an aura of light that enveloped him, and he replied.

"Yeshua, has sent you to free me?"

Henel nodded and replied, "Who the son sets free. Is free indeed. Or I would not have told you. Live free Abba."

Ezra looked behind his son to the door that ever seemed out of reach. He then heard a knock at the door.

Henel moved himself from his father's path. "Go Abba, open the door and let Yeshua enter."

"But I can never seem to reach him… God I mean."

"God will reach for you."

Ezra looked at his son, then at the door behind him. Instantly, a knock gently echoed from the entrance. He strolled towards the door and this time it did not move away from him. Nor did the opening become smaller. He reached for the doorknob and placed his hands on it, and turned it. The door opened and a figure in white stood just outside the entrance and spoke. "Hello, Ezra. I have been waiting a long time to see you."

Ezra smiled, "Please come in."

Like a star that entered a room, light emblazoned over everything Henel's eyes could see and the light was such that its radiance washed out his father and his internal demons from view, and Henel covered his eyes, for the light was too much to behold and he closed them tightly, and put his hands over his face.

The light then diminished and when it did, he removed his hand and Janus stood next to him and they were at the portal to the Gate of Limbus and the angel spoke.

"Well done, Adamson, well done indeed. It would seem that your time here has concluded and Argoth awaits you on the other side to see your way home."

Henel squinted and rubbed his eyes and replied, "What about my father?"

Janus smiled and motioned with his hand towards the gate. "The answers that you seek, Henel, son of James, can no longer be found in the realm of choices. Go and see."

Henel looked at the great azure door before him and stepped through to see where his journey and that of his father would lead.

Prime Realm: The Ancient Past

Lotan watched his brethren follow the Lord into the Gate of Limbo. The great door shown white, then flashed in azure blue until it settled in the incessant churning of its previous state. Lotan stood on the platform of the Tempest Throne and once again the area became dim and Limbo was as before. Quiet save for the whispers of the Mists that were always there but out of sight. He thought of the events that had led them to this point and the words given by the Lord, and he inhaled and sighed. The words of the Lord weighed heavy on him and he turned and spoke to Janus, who was allowed to remain in Limbo and who stood to his side.

"I am sorry that you cannot return home at this time, my brother," said Lotan.

Janus looked at what would now be his new home. It was dark, unlike the brightness that was Heaven. The air was humid and the churning of the gate of Limbo and its temporal storms were more conscious to his mind. He resigned himself to his surroundings, knowing that they would be temporary, and turned to his peer and smiled. "A seal of the Lord has been broken. The portent must be sealed with me until the time of the Lord's judgment is unleashed. The Anti-Christ cannot be allowed to manifest in the Earth before the time appointed. The wrath contained within me must be set aside for now. But it will fall to Argoth to one day dispense the judgments, and to our brethren to break the seals. I will indeed miss the heavenly city. But I am content that I will see it and my fellows again. And what of you?"

Lotan walked over to the obsidian chair and settled into the Tempest Throne. He felt the cold onyx stone armrest of the seat. It was an ugly chair. A seat suitable for a realm the Lord had cordoned off to contain the sin of the Universe.

"I, to look forward to living among my brethren and the humans. For though I was there at the beginning when he made the heavens and the earth. I will again be there when he remakes the same. I, too, hold on to this promise. For I will look for a city which hath foundations, whose builder and maker is God. My stewardship of this realm… my appointment to see the sins of the world displaced here and washed away from existence will one day be complete. And on that day, I will rejoice. Until then, the Mists must be contained, and the realm monitored. But you and I are now here together. To oversee the realm of choices. To know what could have been. To see the alternatives and to know the goings on of how El works all things to one end. How all choices contribute to his design. And to know the refuse of choices that do not."

Janus nodded. "There is a passage from the gate to the basement of Heaven. The door was damaged by both Raphael and the Mists' incursion. The breach must be repaired, no?"

"The tear cannot be repaired. It can only be guarded so that the Mists cannot run amok into the Land of Heaven. And thus, the wisdom of the Lord becomes known. You are the two faced one. Thus, go to Janus, and with thy two faces guard the door that none may escape and guard heaven, that none may enter the realm of Limbo without the seal of El. For as I am warden to watch over the land of choices. You are now warden over the door itself."

Janus nodded and set himself to flight towards the door to the basement of heaven. A door he would guard with his life to prevent the seep of contagion into the realm of Heaven. And when he left Lotan, he in time settled in front of the Gate of Limbo that led to Heaven's cellar. And he erected in the power of the Lord a mirror over the broken door. A gate of Eternal Views. A mirror to face the Mists that they might be frightened by their own visage and dispelled by the horrors of their own existence. A mirror that, when one looked, one would see themselves ad infinitum. A true mirror of horrors to keep the Mists at bay. And Janus unsheathed his sword as a sentry that, if any thought to pass, he was empowered to cut the creatures down. And the Mists set themselves to depart from the place so that they might not be destroyed by the grigori with two faces and a gleaming black sword. For none dared face the wrath of an appointed guard of God. And Janus watched Limbos' movements, for she was alive. And with two faces, he noted the possibilities that slowly, over time, filled the realm of choices. And with his two faces he looked with one set of eyes towards the darkness of the land that contained sin, and with the other: to the light that emanated even from Heaven's basement and so Janus clung to hope… hope that in time the promise of Yeshua would be realized, and he would be released with Lotan that there be no more need to guard a door to a realm of sin.

* * *

Argoth emerged from the Gate of Limbo and when he stepped through, he immediately felt the heat upon his face. It was a thing that caused him to instantly phase to protect himself. But even phased, the heat was relentless and in the midst of the sweltering he heard the multitude of voices cry out to a being that stood in the center of a cavern. For, surrounding him on all sides, were stones set afire. Each element unformed and raw. And yet each rang out aloud a plea to the being that stood within its center. An inquiry 'to be'.

And when Argoth realized where he was, and who was in his presence, he instantly knelt down and forgot about the furnace that raged about him. For consciousness came to him that he stood in the midst of the kiln: the birthplace of angels. And before him was God. And the Holy Spirit spoke to him.

"Rise, Argoth of House Grigori. In you, I am well pleased. Do you know where you are?"

Argoth nodded. "I am in the womb of thy making and the birthplace of my kind. I stand in the Kiln next to my God. A place that only the chief prince has been privy to. I am not worthy to see your doings in the making of our kind my king."

The Holy Spirit replied, "Even if that doing is a rebirth of thee?"

Argoth raised his head in confusion. "My king?"

You, my son, are one who has seen a glimpse of the end and one who has entered outside my command into Limbo. Because of this thing there has been a stirring to the mystery of iniquity and the beginning of the end has now come."

"I do not understand, my Lord. I ask my God for wisdom to understand his words."

"Granted." said the Holy Spirit. The third person of the trinity then waved his hand and two stones sprung up from the floor and into the Lord God's hand. He spoke to Argoth. "Within my palms are Chronos and Kairos. For with Chronos, I will show you the things that will come hereafter. And with Kairos, I will give thee the opportunity to be set right and undo the harm created by your unauthorized entry into Limbo."

The Lord then breathed on the stone of Chronos and it grew like one of the black pulsating globules that hovered within the throne room of the Tempest Throne.

And it shimmered with white energy, and something broke free from the ebony orb. And there was an image, and the image was one of Lucifer and behind him was a third of heaven's might that followed. And he had turned into a dragon such that his form was unrecognizable. And the Dragon and his angels fought with Michael and his angels. And the battle was such that Raphael was struck down and Jerahmeel awakened Argoth, who, with his help, showed the deceitfulness of his brother. And Argoth saw Lucifer was allowed to smite the heel of El and blood came from the wound and, with his blood, it flowed into Limbo to create a new reality. And the fourth race God had created also fell into sin. And the whole of Creation was brought under bondage by the Withering so that El himself would send the Lord Yeshua to redeem the Clayborn from the wages of their sin. And upon Yeshua's triumphant return to heaven. His blood was presented to God and then taken and poured as a sacrifice over the Tempest Throne, which served as an altar. And life was given to Limbo, but not before the Anti-Christ who they had witnessed was allowed to ravage the Earth below. And Argoth watched in fear and trembling as the wrath of the Lord mounted upon the people of the Earth and that Yeshua took captive in a final battle that great dragon and cast him alive, and all that raised themselves in rebellion into a lake of fire. And at the end, the Lord created a new Heaven and a new Earth and all things were made new. And then the image stopped and grew dark.

And Argoth was panting, for the images were such that he could barely comprehend what was played before him. But he knew he saw the future, though none of the events had transpired. He realized that Limbo was simply the waterfall of possibilities, but what the Lord God showed him was the dispensation of time that had been willed to come.

He shook his head. "Is this because we entered Limbo my king?"

"No, my son. But because thou hast entered with thy Grigoric brethren, the realm now has three Sephiroths. This cannot be. For the image can only be contained by one. Therefore thou has been brought here: to the time of thy birth, to go forth a second time until the time appointed where you can be Sephiroth and fulfill the call for which thou hast been called."

"After... Raphael's death?"

"Aye," said the Lord.

"And until then?"

"Thou art silenced from speaking, but shall be a totem for

all who look upon thee in wonder to consider that there is nothing covered that shall not be revealed. For this mercy I give thee to retain what thou hast seen. To know what shall come but unable to share. But to witness the cause of creation when my people deviate from my will. Mercy, for all things I weave towards the purpose of my will. Even this and even thee. I will not remove thy stone. But you shall witness the removal of many for thy trespass against the command of God. And thou shalt be rewound to the time of thy birth from the Kiln. But despair not, for my promise I give to thee that thou shalt again rejoin thy two brethren at the end."

Argoth understood and bowed his head in submission to his king. "Let it be according to thy word, my King."

"Now go," said the Lord. "And I will allow thee words before thou art silenced for a time."

Argoth then turned from the Lord Pneuma. And God opened an exit from the Kiln and when he did all those exterior to the mountain of God turned their heads for God was ready to reveal one of their number into being, and all wondered of what house would the angel be. And a flame shot from the mouth of the mountain and all saw that a grigori exited and shouts of praise was given for the mighty house of Grigori; for one had been added to their number. And as was the custom of all Grigori when they exited the Kiln and before they phased past the vision of angelic site, they would make an announcement and all Heaven waited for the angel of house Grigori to speak. And El Pneuma appeared before him and proclaimed, "Behold my servant Argoth, one of the great ones of Grigoric kind." And Argoth's words were recorded on this wise.

Argoth then walked to the edge of the mountain of the Lord. He looked at the beauty of the Lord and understood the mercy and severity of the same, and a tear welled from his eye for the magnanimity of his God. For so overwhelmed with the love and the wisdom of his king that he gritted his teeth and looked out over the expanse of the Kingdom of Heaven, and proclaimed,

"The LORD, The LORD God, merciful and gracious, long-suffering, and abundant in goodness and truth. Keeping mercy for thousands, forgiving iniquity and transgression and sin, and that will by no means clear the guilty, visiting the iniquity of the fathers upon the children and upon the children's children, unto the third and to the fourth generation."

And El Pneuma nodded after this proclamation, then the Lord said to him, "For nothing is secret that shall not be made manifest; neither anything hid that shall not be made known." El Pneuma immediately silenced him, and the cliffs were muzzled from echoing what Argoth had uttered. And all of heaven was astonished for the sounds which emanated from the cliffs because of the various flora and fauna that lived below could no longer be heard and the place was quiet, as if stricken dumb. And all of Heaven wondered at the thing.

    And many went to speak to Argoth because he did not phase invisible as other Grigori, but he did not speak nor look at any, but in time he made himself towards the Great Library and he sat himself outside the steward's room. And those that finally noted where he settled swore that a tear rolled down his eye. For occasionally it was said he turned his head towards the reference room of the Great Library. As if he waited…. waited for something to yet take place. And the spot where Argoth would not move came to be known as Kairos. For Argoth stood himself atop a pedestal and no more moved. For all waited when the opportunity would come for the angel to display the greatness El Pneuma had proclaimed.

    Thus, Argoth stood silently with outstretched hands just outside the reference room of the Great Library. And when no one looked, he turned his face to eye a small book in the center of the room underneath the stained glass dome. A book that oozed a mist similar to what he had witnessed in Limbo. And he knew the black book and on its spine in gilded gold was titled, 'Tome of Iniquity'. And a tear welled up in his eye. For here he would wait for events to catch up to what the Lord had shown him: for here he would wait for Raphael to die so that he might live a second time.

Theta Realm. The Ancient Past

Lucifer and Michael stepped from the dimensional rift that was the Gate of Limbo. Lucifer exited first, then Michael instantly followed. The air was stale, ancient pillars towered overhead, and all were carved with the handwriting of El up and down each one.

"I see the energies of the Tempest Throne flows even here," said Michael.

"Wherever, here is." replied Lucifer.

"Indeed." was Michael's reply.

For a moment, the gate's energy churned behind them and then dissipated into nothing. Leaving the duo surrounded in darkness akin to twilight.

"Perhaps we can return?" said Lucifer.

"Yeshua made it clear that we were to remain here until the appointed time."

"Pfsst," said Lucifer. "The only reason I even entered the realm was to protect the will of Yeshua. And now I stand here condemned for seeking to enforce his will. Where is the justice to sentence me to solitary confinement? It is not justice, I say." Lucifer kicked a rock and eyed the dankness of the place.

Michael replied, "I too have disobeyed the Lord. His edict

was clear yet was defied. We are fortunate that the punishment was not more severe."

Lucifer illuminated himself to increase the level of light in the chamber. As he did, the fog that surrounded them moved away and they could see the slithering of small hands and feet scamper away. And voices that whispered retreated deeper into the darkness.

"Perhaps," said Lucifer. "But the way of the Lord is not equal Michael. Were there not thousands that obeyed my voice? Yet here I stand… alone. Alone in the dark with nothing but the dross vile of sin to accompany me. The way of the Lord I say is not equal."

Michael looked at his brother in pity. "You are not alone, brother. You have me."

Lucifer returned Michael's look and replied. "I would suppose you would think that should comfort me. I would not be here if it were not for you."

Michael drew his neck back from his brother's words and his face drew taunt in anger and offense.

"Me? You blame me?" Michael raised his voice, and he was incredulous. "Was it not I who advised thee to leave the Grigori alone? Was it not I who told thee that if we continue in this trial, I dare say we risk fracturing the Lumazi. Who was it that asked if we had enough breaches already with the Schism: a rupture which you were the cause? And in my concern over further separation with the

Ophanim and the Seraphim, I myself am now found separated from my king for seventy years. Bound to be in the company of one who cannot even bring himself to recognize his own part in his confinement. You are a curse, Lucifer Draco, a lustful blight whose allegiance is to thyself alone. 'I am the Chief Prince and I too am also appointed by God. My will is law.' Do you remember those words? You are nothing but a child spoiled. And I will not follow one who cannot even confess his own errant way." Michael then turned from Lucifer and walked away.

Lucifer was stung by his brother's words and became incensed and replied, "You will not talk to me that way! I am the Chief Prince and I walk among the Stones of Fire!" He then flew to his brother and grabbed him by the shoulder, turned him around to face him, and struck him with his palm across his face.

Michael's cheek became red from the strike and he returned a backhanded blow to his brother's face, knocking the angel backward to his rear.

Lucifer wiped blood from his lip and unsheathed his sword. Michael did the same.

Lucifer then detonated in blinding light and Michael, ready for his barrage, raised his arm as a shield to protect his eyes. And the two angels fought with one another. For the love of brothers had turned to hate. And thus the words of Raphael-Chi rang in the memory of Michael's mind and was now fulfilled that the love of Michael would turn to ash; and "for the hatred wherewith you shall hate, shall be greater than the love wherewith you once loved."

And their hatred seethed in the darkness of Limbo whilst around them eyes from the blackness stared at their rage. Eyes of yellow that were attached to creatures that were choices contrary to God. Ghostly manifestations of sin and the discarded shells of failed love towards God and the brethren. For deep in the darkness, they watched gleefully as the two angels fought with one another. For pride was a sin that was ripe to birth other iniquity into the realm of reality. Therefore, the Mists would watch as these two shed sin in the land of Limbo. Watch as they whispered to one another in ecstatic delight at the actions set before them: actions that nourished them. And with that satiation, they would whisper the refrain that was known throughout Limbo. A warning… and a plea to yield to temptation.

"Feed the Mists."

* * *

Lilith walked into the Gate of Limbo and when he did a long prismatic tunnel seemed to move further away, and when he looked to his rear to see if the gate of limbo was still open. He saw that the Lord God Yeshua was behind him and walked behind him and a sword was in his mouth as if he hunted the angel. And Lilith, eying the Lord, sought to flee, but the exit from Limbo simply moved further away. And as he ran from the Lord, the words of the King of Kings followed him like birds that harassed the head of an escaping man.

"Hear me, oh rebellious one. You failed to abide in thy calling and was not content to record the greatest of my sons. And in your desire to lift thyself to be Chief of Eyes, thou hast created a future apart from me and have sought to escape the fate that awaits you. And in your foolishness, you have unleashed my adversary before his time.

And because thou hast done this thing, thou shalt abide in the seal of thy fear. To be aware yet unable to change that which is to come. You will be the lying spirit I will use to bring to the surface that which must now come.

For you have become dross, therefore, behold, I am going to gather you into the midst of Jerusalem. As they gather silver and bronze and iron and lead and tin into the furnace to blow fire on it in order to melt it, so I will gather you in My anger and in My wrath and I will lay you there and melt you. I will gather you and blow on you with the fire of my wrath, and you will be melted in the midst of it.

You will be the instrument to remove the dross that my

son might be removed. All the while knowing that in doing so you merely hasten thine own demise. Lie to thyself, lie that the truth might be known.

For ye have set at naught all my counsel, and would none of my reproof: I also will laugh at your calamity; I will mock when your fear cometh; When your fear cometh as desolation, and your destruction cometh as a whirlwind; when distress and anguish cometh upon you. Then shall you call upon me, but I will not answer; you shall seek me early, but shall not find me: For thou hast hated knowledge, and did not choose the fear of the Lord: nor abide my counsel: thou hast despised all my reproof. Therefore, because thou hast played the fool and released the Anti-Christ into the realm before his time. The spirit of Antichrist will be thy king.

For thou hast traveled up and down the spine of eternity with a God stone. And now you shall eat of the fruit of thine own way, and be filled with their own devices."

"My lord, my sentence is too much for me for all that know what I have done will smite me."

"Nay, for I will give sleep of mind to those that know of thy collusion, until it will be manifest what thou art. And then when you have thought to have escaped from my hand, when thy pride hast blossomed; then thou shalt eat the fruit of thy labor and dissolution will befall you."

Lilith then found himself outside the gate of Limbo and he arrived with a breeze and found himself near his charge, Lucifer. And Lucifer had just dismissed the angelic council he had established on Earth to build the great city of Athor and after everyone had departed Lucifer, he sat by himself alone to review several scrolls he had in hand.

Lilith then floated invisibly near to him, stood in front of him and then slowly revealed himself so that the angel might see him and spoke.

"Greetings Chief Prince, I am Lilith and have been assigned to chronicle thee by God himself."

Lucifer looked up, surprised to see his Grigori, and replied. "Indeed? But why reveal yourself to me, let alone announce yourself to me? Is this not against the rule of the Grigori? Is something amiss?"

Lilith smirked, "I am… allowed to extend the rule of the Grigori. A spirit unique to thee that it might be seen what is found in thee. I possess the desire to move beyond what has been granted to me. I sense you desire this as well. In time I will show you that perhaps one day we might both be free of the predestined plans given to us."

Lucifer placed his scrolls away and warily eyed the angel. "You speak words that are beyond my thoughts. I am the Chief

Prince of Almighty God. I am above all things and second to God himself. I am beauty and the sound of beauty personified. What more would I as Chief Prince desire or could be offered to me?"

Lilith nodded, "What more indeed, for what else is there save to be God himself? And if thou be a Son of God, what then must a son grow to be, but a father himself?"

And Lucifer scoffed at the angel's words, "You would think me to be God?"

Lilith misted and as he faded, he replied to the Chief Prince. "Thou sayest it." He then hid himself behind the veil of angelic sight.

And the words of Lilith would not leave Lucifer, and he pondered the thing in his heart.

* * *

Raphael walked into the throne room, sat before his king, and looked at the enormous book within his hands: a tome that contained all the information the Lord El had requested.

"My Lord, the task wherewith I have been charged is complete. I have tallied all as thou hast commanded."

El looked upon Raphael and smiled, "And what did your examination find, my son?"

Raphael's face became angst-ridden. His heart and mind

were burdened by what he knew, the knowledge he must now dispense to the Lord. Never had he given the Lord a negative report. Now he must be the first Elohim to broach the subject of treason with his king.

"My Lord, your instruction was to find all instances of thought, conduct, and or speech similar to Abaddon's. To bring to you a concise volume that lists all Elohim and the result of my findings."

El saw that Raphael's lip tightened and that the cherubim struggled to choke back tears.

"Raphael, speak my son, for there is nothing covered that shall not be revealed and hid that shall not be made known. Fear not."

Raphael straightened himself, wiped his eyes, cleared his throat and spoke as directed.

"Lord, of the host of Heaven there is a number whose mind is pure and whose fealty my King can command without question. Those whose names are written therein are not so. They number almost a third of Heaven. Those who dissent to thy rule speak of displeasure with Abaddon's sentence, the existence of Hell, or take issue with relations with the humans. They say that the humans are not Kilnborn, not of the Stones of Fire. There are some who are displeased to serve a creature of mud and clay."

"And what of the Grigori?" asked El.

"My God, again the Grigori as a whole are with thee my king, yet it pains me to report that all are not so. I regret that I have yet to determine the extent to which my own kind has departed from the way."

"I do know that entries of several tomes have made me concerned. There are records, which seem to do more than simply state the observations that the Grigori have heard or seen. I have found several Grigori whose records have added commentary to their accounts. Some no longer seem content to only document the observations of their charge but to annotate as well."

Raphael looked away from the Lord and paused.

"Continue, do not hold back that which thou hast found." said El.

"I have traced the genesis of this corruption, my king. Moreover, I am afraid that one of the Lumazi is the seed to the fruit from which all springs. In a review of which tomes no longer hold true, they point back to one Grigori. Lilith and his tomes are no longer valid, thus out of the mouth of two or three must they now be established. In a review of the tome of Lilith on the Chief Prince, I have seen an entry that hast given me pause.

Lilith's entry was not journaled in accordance to Grigoric law, but because the Grigori are abundant in number; another was in proximity at the time and revealed an inconsistency.

"I believe this entry is the accurate one my Lord, and that which I present now to thy light: the copy of which I hold in my hand. Its record compels me to further investigate any new additions in Lilith's accord of Lucifer."

"And the entry; what did it contain my son?"

Raphael tossed the book into the air, and the voluminous work stood vertically, as if coming to attention. The manuscript separated into cover and pages; its sheets flew across the throne, and the pages assembled themselves so that the recorded journal entry was chronologically on top.

Light glowed on the first page. It floated higher to touch the ceiling, and the image of Lucifer and Lilith walking in the Garden of Eden appeared. A Grigori assigned to watch a flock of sheep observed the occurrence and documented a portion of the unauthorized conversation.

"And what is thy desire, Chief Prince? What would satisfy you?"

Lucifer looked skyward. His eyes aimed upward as if he gazed directly at God and Raphael.

"That I might ascend into Heaven; that my throne would be exalted above the stars of God.

That I would sit also upon the mount of the congregation,

in the sides of the north: To ascend above the heights of the clouds..."

The image then dissipated, and the mammoth book flared with a flash of white light, reassembled itself, and then fell with a loud thump to the floor.

El stood, Raphael kneeled, silently waiting for any command from his Lord. Then El spoke. "Go, Raphael. Summon thy brothers as there is much to do, the seventh-day approaches, and I must take rest from all my labor."

"Yes, my lord." Raphael bowed, picked up the book, and turned to walk away. Leaving the sanctuary through one of the many side chambers, Raphael returned to his home within the mountain itself. He walked through the corridor of Mt. Zion and entered the Great Hall of Annals.

He passed by multiple stacks and shelves of records and books until he came to a desk, sat, and placed the completed tome he had just recently finished down; it hit the stone slab of the desk with a thud.

He looked over and noticed that Lucifer's tome was still recording. New information was penned in angelic script. The letters were in flames, and Raphael's eyes fixated on one passage that leaped off the page.

Raphael's eyes grew wide and his mouth opened, but his

tongue could not form words.

His mind raced with thoughts and then froze in disbelief and panic as he lifted the book and reread each new passage. Hope dashed away as he read, and the horrible truth dawned on him with each sentence, words that he knew somehow would forever change creation.

'I will be like the most High.'

And Raphael sighed within himself. For with the vision, he realized that the future he had seen through the veins of Limbo was the beginning of the end and that he witnessed nothing more than a portent of falling stars.

Epilogue

The Prime Realm the Future

Ezra James opened his eyes.

And when he did, he heard the alarms of machines that had connected him to monitor his vitals and to keep him alive.

He turned his head to see various IVs hooked into his arm.

A woman walked in, a nurse. Clipboard in hand, she checked the machine's readings and noted that her patient looked at her.

Her clipboard fell to the floor, and the startled cry of surprise mixed with excitement was carried in her yelp.

"Oh My God Mr. James. You are awake! Can you hear me?"

Ezra nodded weakly.

"Let me go get the doctor he will want to see you right away!" She turned to leave when Ezra reached and grabbed her arm before she could depart and spoke.

"My son was just here. Where is he?"

* * *

Argoth watched as the gate to Limbo shimmered. Its glowing aura indicated that someone or something was coming. A figure then appeared, and a man stepped from the blue gate of Limbo into Heaven. Henel James had returned from his journey and the human smiled when he set eyes upon his angelic guide.

"Welcome back Mr. James," said Argoth.

Henel replied, "My father… is he well?"

"Yes, Mr. James. He is well. I have received a report that your journey was a success. Congratulations Mr. James. It would seem the Lord's confidence in you was not misplaced. I will escort you back to the way point as I'm sure you are eager to be reunited with your father." Argoth then turned to go, expecting Henel would follow.

But Henel paused and stared at the gate, and rehearsed in his mind the things he had seen. He then took a hold of Argoth's arm and held it. "Wait…"

Argoth turned his head. "Adamson?"

"My father… he is well?"

"Yes," replied Argoth. "He is expected to make a full recovery."

"And he is written in the Lamb's book of life?" said Henel.

Argoth nodded. "The thing is, as you say. But why the questions Adamson, are you not ready to return?"

Henel turned back towards the Gate of Limbo and replied. "Because there is so much possibility within Limbo. I would like to see what could have been. Like to see what was. You have given me the opportunity to explore, not just history. But to travel to see what *could* have been history. It is an explorer's dream, and a journalist's ambition. I cannot think of anyone in all of human history who has ever been presented with such an opportunity."

"Always the journalist Mr. James. If you were not human, I would think that you are an angel of House Grigori. Even now the Lord God has consented you access to create this tome of yours. You should feel honored to be given leave to traverse the land of Limbo."

Henel bowed slightly at the compliment and replied. "You honor me sir." He then looked at Argoth and asked him. "If I go, how long would I be gone and how much time do I have to explore?"

Argoth looked at him and the chronograph that the human had adorned on his wrist and said. "Until the Lord remakes all of Heaven and Earth."

Henel, not understanding having never finished his reading of the biblical scrolls, replied. "And how long is that?"

Argoth smiled as he turned to walk away, leaving the man at the gate of limbo. "A thousand years, Adamson. I will await your return in a thousand years so that we might continue our conversation. But for you… your journey will no doubt seem like a day. Do not concern yourself with your father. I will send an emissary who will explain your decision to him. However, knowing Ezra, he will undoubtedly understand, and I suppose it is not like you will not have eternity for the two of you to catch up."

Henel smiled.

Argoth continued, "You are indeed your father's son and I am sure he would be proud of the man you have become."

Henel once again bowed slightly at the compliment and also knew his father well enough to know he would probably chastise him extensively for not availing himself of the opportunity to explore. Besides, it would give them much to talk about. Henel then looked at the glowing gate of light and its iridescent blue beckoned him to enter. Fog crept from it and he noted it wound up the stairs and slowly consumed and darkened all things. He began to slowly understand. Understand that El had finally given Lotan leave to complete the consummation of this realm, that the Mists would no longer be held back, and that in a thousand years God would create a new heaven and a new earth. He also knew he would have to hurry, for a thousand years would pass as a day. The epiphany did not surprise him; in fact, a deeper understanding was dawning on him. He looked to Argoth and entered when he saw the angel stop and also look at him.

"Please tell Andel that I will be back soon."

Argoth nodded, "I will… besides, for him: you will only be gone for a day."

Henel chuckled in reply and turned from Argoth and stepped back into the Gate of Limbo. The azure gate flashed and the human's form was seen no more.

A figure then also materialized within the gate. The being had the similitude of a man, but a crown made of lightning was upon his head and he stepped through the barrier to the realms to gaze upon Argoth, who stood waiting at the stairs leading up towards the main concourse of the palace.

The face was that of the ancient and familiar face

of Lotan: a face Argoth had not seen for many of Heaven's days.

"It has been a long time, Argoth," Lotan said.

Argoth nodded. "Indeed. I trust the human is assured safety within your realm?"

Lotan smiled. "All are safe until El decrees the end of this age. And then I will be free: free to do the work assigned to me." Lotan smiled and recited the words of the ancient biblical scroll back to Argoth's hearing. *"For, in the beginning, God created the heaven and the earth. And the earth was without form, and void; and darkness was upon the face of the deep. And the Spirit of God moved upon the face of the waters.* And soon….He shall release me, and at his word I shall purge creation itself from the taint of sin. And then, then El shall begin again."

Argoth looked upon Lotan. Looked upon this primordial creation of God. He who Leto Alexander had sought to unleash against the whole of Creation prior to El's elected timing. A force of obliteration that was restrained and off limits to all: a being housed within the domain of Limbo.

Argoth looked into the eyes of this ancient being. The unspoken father of House Grigori and a creature who was almost as timeless as El himself… almost. Argoth peered into the white eyes of Lotan: the name that angels had once given the King of Limbo. But Argoth was Sephiroth and knew his true name… understood the true nature of this being that stared back at him and with whom Raphael had bartered with so long ago. A name that Lucifer had once learned from Lilith. A name he would not say aloud for the time of Lotan's coming was not yet nigh: a time that would precede the new world that was prophesied. For as he had done before; God would issue forth command, and from his mouth matter would form: but not before. Not before the command to remove the old. For the old would assuredly pass away. And Argoth looked upon the personification of the nothingness that would exist between the tick and tock of El's word, and he beheld he who upon God's nod would bring about the cessation of all things. The ancient one. The true name of Lotan.

The Void.

The End

Grigoric Glossary of Terms: Scroll Three
To: Henel James
From: Argoth

To wit, the Lord hath given me word to make thee understand by scrolls the ways of Heaven. I have determined it incumbent to tutor thee of the races that populate her midst. Know that though thy people hath acquired some information through observation and encounters with our kind, there is yet much that thou must still learn. This scroll hath been prepared for thy reading and translated from our tongue that ye might grasp our number. I will expand upon your instruction in future lessons. As you hast advanced in learning, I have now amended thy scroll to provide thee access into the tomes of the great houses, and Celestial history concerning the Schism, and the Articles of War which governs our kind.

Commit the knowledge given to study and see my attendant if thou dost require additional resources.

Note: It hath been brought to my attention that thou hast made inquiry regarding the Books of Seals which El hast commissioned me to prepare. Note that this book is for El alone, and He will reveal it at His choosing.

Furthermore, your request to access tomes concerning the Mists, the Ophanim, and the Seraphim have been denied by El Pneuma. His word He would have me relay to you, and I quote, "The anointing which ye have received of Me abideth in thee, and ye need not that any man teach thee: but as the same anointing teacheth thee of all things, and is truth and is no lie, and even as it hath been taught thee, thou shalt abide in Him."

I trust that these words will give you contentment. Please, do not let them fall to the ground.

Your servant appointed by His grace in the understanding of our ways,

Argoth Grigori

The Chief of Eyes, and Sephiroth of House Grigori.

El or Jehovah

The name angels have given to God and by which He has revealed Himself to them. Triune in nature, El is often seen in a singular bodily form. On rare occasions, His triune nature is revealed as three separate distinct personalities (Father, Son, and Holy Ghost); collectively they are called the Godhead.

Elohim

The collective name of all celestial kind in Biblical lore; also called the Sons of God. Elohim are distinct from Yeshua, who is the only Begotten Son. Let it be known that Grigoric trances have shown that righteous men will also be adopted into the family of God. This knowledge is not yet commonly known among the people.

The Schism

An event in Heavenly history that caused the separation of the three celestial races, attributed to Lucifer's trafficking to elevate the Elohim above the Ophanim and Seraphim.

The Descension

The day noted by all angelic-kind that Lucifer was thrown out of Heaven.

Godhead

The Trinity composed of the Father (El), the Son (Yeshua), and the Holy Ghost (El Pneuma).

Chief Prince

An honorific title given to one of seven angelic princes who stands before the presence of God and receives instructions for his race. The Chief Prince is entrusted by El to walk within the Stones of Fire and to protect the secret of the chamber, the Primestone... a repository of God's power where one may become as God. Michael stands as Chief Prince of Angels. Lucifer formerly held this rank. This rank is not to be confused with the Angel of the Lord, who is Yeshua.

Lumazi (Re 4:5)

The group of seven archangels who stand before the throne of God. They are the chief angelic council that executes the will of God in the universe. The head of each major house is represented on the council. The seven houses are Malakim, Kortai, Draco, Issi, Arelim, Grigori, and Harrada.

Ladder (aka Orphanic Portal) (Ge 28:12)

A mode of transport utilized by angels to travel between realms. Ladders are created by the Ophanim. Angels simply travel in the wake that the celestial beings create as they move from place to place.

Limbo

Also known as the Realm of Choices. An in-between place. The land between life and death. The land of infinite possibilities. Limbo is placed in the basement of Heaven, yet above the Maelstrom of the Abyss. It is the only passage to the other side of the Mountain of God that leads to the land of the Seraphim, as well as other regions of Heaven. El hath restricted full access to this area's tome.

Tartarus (2 Peter 2:4)

A prison designed by Lucifer to dispose of those who opposed him. Presently it is in use by the Lord as a holding cell until He has determined their end.

Ashe

The legendary city of fire and home of the Seraphim. A metropolis made of living fire. The city is located in the land of Aesir.

Hell

A living mountain that serves as a prison. Designed originally with angels in mind, it lives off the eternal spirit of Elomic flesh. It possesses the ability to reproduce similar to an amoeba and can grow. Grigoric spies indicate that Hell has grown to hold captive humans. (Isa 5:14 Therefore hell hath enlarged herself, and opened her mouth without measure: and their glory, and their multitude, and their pomp, and he that rejoiceth shall descend into it.)

Scouts indicate that humans now abide in two compartments within the creature. Hades: the realm of the unrighteous dead. Paradise: The realm of the righteous dead. Prior to Yeshua's resurrection, Paradise was the place where the righteous dead were held in the spirit realm until they were freed. These two domains were separated by a gulf that prevented residents from crossing to one another.

(Luke 16:26)

Shiloah

The title angels have given the man who can defeat Lucifer.

Dissolution

"Death" to a celestial being is called dissolution.

The Kiln

A furnace from which El created all celestial life and the former storehouse of the Stones of Fire; the living elements of creation. At the heart of the Kiln was the Primestone, and the ultimate test for angelic kind.

Elomic Command

A vowel, consonant, or phrase allowing the power of God to be invoked.

The Abyss

A gulf of nether sometimes referred to by thy kind as Limbo or by daemon kind as "the wilderness." It is a realm that separates the Third and Second Heavens. Failure to bridge the realms without a Ladder or direct intervention from El can cause one to be entrapped within the winds of the nether.

The winds are referred to as the Maelstrom. Kortai builders frequently build near the edge of the Maelstrom to expand the landscape of Heaven. The Abyss is also referred to as the "bottomless pit."

Mortals cannot pass through the Abyss without shedding their corporeal shell. Only Death or direct translation by God allows passage past the Abyss into the spiritual world of Heaven. El hath mentioned that He may release this tome to thee at a later time.

Waypoint

A designated area where travel between two points was allowed by God. Failure to utilize a waypoint could displace the Third Heaven with the second or vice versa, causing untold destruction.

Grigoric Trance

A vision given by God to some Grigori who are able on occasion to see one generation ahead into the future.

Manna

The food that angels consume. Grown in the fields of Elysium, it is shipped to the four corners of creation to supply angels with sustenance. When harvested, it instantly grows back. During the exodus of the children of Israel, the nation temporarily fed on this food. (Exodus 16:15)

Cadmime/cadmium

A black crystal-like mineral created by God. It is a living thing that grows similar to human bones. It is the hardest, most durable substance known to angelic kind. The substance is used to undergird the basement of heaven and her foundations. It can stretch and grow as directed. It is extremely pliable and able to be made into a variety of substances, from building materials to weapons of war.

The Burning

The Burning is a process that the Seraphim may engage where all Seraphim may unite as one single entity. All who participate while in this state are able to know and share one another's thoughts.

Their collective flame is equivalent to the flames of Hell or the former Kiln. There are few things that can survive if the collective body of Seraphim fires.

Creatures

Cherubim

A type of angel having great power; but not necessarily governmental oversight.

Seraphim

A heavenly creature designed to serve as a voice to the holiness of God; also called a "Burning One." A creature of great power.

There are four which stand at the temple of God. The rest of the Seraphim have not been seen since the great Schism and are kept behind the mountain of God in the land of Aesir.

The Seraphim appear as floating fire with flaming eyes and wings in their natural state and assume a humanoid form when in the presence of others. When they do so, their voices can create sounds that defy the hearing. El hath restricted full access to their tome.

Virtue

A living sentient aroma that lives before the throne of God and perfumes the throne. El hath restricted full access to their tome.

Ophanim (Ezekiel 1:15-21)

A heavenly creature designed to serve as guard to the presence of God. They are also movers of planetary and star systems. El hath restricted full access to their tome.

Zoa (Rev. 4:1-9 5:1- 6:1)

A heavenly creature designed to serve as guard to the secret things of God.

Stones of Fire (Eze 28:14)

A living sentient element which can be molded in the Kiln to create celestial life. They are also called Kilnstones or Godstones.

Shekinah Glory

The residue of God's breath, equivalent to the exhaling of a human's carbon dioxide; a living cloak of breathing light that envelops and irradiates the person of God. Primarily, a localized phenomenon. Those that come near the Lord are irradiated by the Shekinah, leaving an afterglow on their own person for a temporary period. The Shekinah can manifest wherever the holiness and righteousness of God exist.

Aithon

The famed flaming horses of Aesir. These great animals pull the fiery chariots of Seraphim riders and were the steeds used to bring Elijah into Heaven. Those that are tamed are stalled in the great flaming city of Ashe.

The Mists

The spiritual living manifestation of sin and choices contrary to God. Limbo is the resident home of these choices. A repository allowed by the Lord until the realm can be emptied into the Lake of Fire when El creates a new Heaven and Earth.

Angelic Rankings

Chief Prince

El's designated angelic leader over all Elohim

The First of Angels/The Sum of all Things (Ez 28:12,13)

An honorific title given to Lucifer

High Prince

Seven angels in existence who speak collectively for all their kind. (Collectively, they are called the Lumazi and are sometimes referred to individually with that honorific title.)

Archon

A sole high-ranking governing angel who directs a specific assignment or regions of territory(s). Sometimes referred to by humans as archangels. The highest-ranking angel over an assignment.

Principality

A sole mid-ranking governing angel who administers more than one territory.

Powers

The lowest ranking governing angel overseeing one territory.

Prime

A non-governing angel representative of a particular virtue. (I.e., love, justice, etc.) After the fall, some angels were designated as prime evils.

Minister

A non-governing angel who serves the cause of El

Daemon

A fallen non-governing angel who serves the cause of Lucifer. Daemons are the regurgitated angelic souls of Hell, released by he who holds the keys to Death and Hell.

Daemons are but shadows of their former angelic selves and

thrive off men, as their Kilnstones have been digested by Hell. Now they seek to inhabit the souls of men, that they might find expression through them.

Specter

Fallen Grigori sometimes referred to by humans as Ghosts.

Shaun-tea'll

A group of angelic warrior dispatched to dispense the judgment of the Lord

The Great Angelic Houses of Heaven

House Draco: Sigil: A dragon

House Draco is the first house of angels and is considered to be highborn in the angelic cast. All Draco are angels of praise and represent beauty, wisdom, and art. Lucifer, prior to his fall, was their represented leader and the firstborn of all angels.

Each Draco has within him the ability to generate sound; some Draco are specifically limited to areas of sound. For example, some Draco can generate all notes within the soprano range, other in the tenor, bass, and alto, but they cannot generate sounds outside the range created. Lucifer is not so and can create any sound.

All Draco have a shimmering translucent skin that allows them to reflect light and therefore project images. They can project certain wavelengths of the spectrum. Each Draco is unique in that they are limited to certain areas of the spectrum. Lucifer, as their leader, is not so limited and may project any image. He may even disappear from view if he chooses to cloak himself in light and be invisible to the eye.

Metatron has now succeeded Lucifer as Prince of his people. Draco, when they choose to be visible to humans, reveal themselves as winged serpents.

Harrada: Sigil: An owl

The House Harrada are considered great sages of wisdom and lore, meticulous in their desire to create order and excel in the development of systems management and the written word.

Each member of house Harrada is adept at manipulating the elements, including heat, air, water, and earth. Also known as lovers of writing, they often create great literary works. Jerahmeel represents the embodiment of the Harrada. Prior to the Descension, God used Jerahmeel to temper Lucifer's tendency toward arrogance.

Harada are keepers of order within all three realms of creation and also exercise control over time and seasons. Harrada is often the head or manager of Heaven's day-to-day operations, including the harvesting of manna. Other angels of this house include Zeus and Chronos.

Kortai: Sigil: A Hammer

The Kortai is a race of builders, muscular and adept in the manipulation of metallurgy and woodworking, minerals and gems. They are the ultimate engineers and constructors of Heaven. Curious to a fault, they have no qualms about delving into new architectural endeavors. It was the Kortai that volunteered to work against the Maelstrom to expand Heaven.

Kortai have a youthful appearance and are incredibly strong in spite of their smaller stature. The Kortai are the engineers of Heaven and are able to bring into creation whatever can be conceived. Michael, the archangel, is the leader of this house. Since the war, they carry a hammer on one side of their belt and a sword in the other, ready to either build or fight at a moment's notice.

Assumably, all that left Heaven did so out of outright rebellion, but those Kortai that left went to see something new, thinking that more than what El had shown them existed, and they were moved to build something apart from El's designs. These are the builders of the Hellforge and the deep chasms that run throughout Hell. Lucifer has silently been turning the Kortai into daemons.

Grigori: Sigil: Two Eyes, a flame, an inkhorn, and stylus

The Grigori are chroniclers: They see all and record all. There are those who chronicle on behalf of God and those who chronicle on behalf of Satan. At least one Grigori records for God at all times. The watchers strive for perfection when documenting the events of history, but regardless of how they view God, their only motive is to chronicle as God designed them this way.

Those who chronicle for Satan say God's actions were not justified and therefore deserves to be overthrown. In the end, they believe their efforts will vindicate their belief in Satan's cause. They give commentary and chronicle with bias, or with an agenda that attempts to besmirch God. They do not simply chronicle…they editorialize. Their purpose for being is to compose. They may not, however, interfere with that which they behold. Those who attempt to harm them are themselves harmed. The Chief Prince is the exception, as he is embodied with authority and power over all angels.

Grigori cannot be stopped nor interfered with without penalty of Abyssian or Tartarus confinement. They can interact with their own kind.

Grigori do not possess the common instruments associated with sight and hearing as they are naturally blind and deaf. They can see as well as anyone and can hear equally well, but they can see nothing but El. They hover, cloaked in purple hoods, and no one has ever seen their face. They have immunity from harm and are able to move freely within both spheres of engagement.

Formerly, Raphael was the prince that oversaw this house but was killed by the fall of Kilnstones during the civil war. Argoth is now the Chief of Eyes and Sephiroth of his house. A few of the Grigori have been gifted with the 'sight', the ability to see beyond what is written to that which shall be written. El has limited this ability; thus, Grigori can only see one generation ahead. When the Grigori use this ability, they go into a trance-like state and attempt to articulate the visions they see.

When El gives a prophecy to a prophet, He speaks to the prophet and allows the Grigori that shadows him to see ahead in time. Angels from this house include Argoth, Hadriel, and Lilith, prior to his dissolution.

Arelim: Sigil: A bull's face

Arelim are strong angels who have the faces of bulls and cloven feet. They can be extremely aggressive in that they enjoy forms of competition. Highly driven by order and authority, yet always seeking to be first in every endeavor, they constantly use their great powers to move planets and power suns.

Able to manipulate the forces of gravity, El has used them to fling planets and keep orbits. Headed by Talus, many of those that left to follow Lucifer were of this house. Proud and strong, they comprise over half of Lucifer's force, making his numbers, though smaller than Heaven, equally formidable in power, for in his ranks reside some of the most powerful of angels. Other angels from this house include Apollyon, aka Abbaddon, Marduk, and Sasheal.

Issi: Sigil: A butterfly

Issi are lovers of beauty, and their gifts allow one to touch anything and manipulate its color. They are also creatures of light, typically soft-spoken, they are humanoid yet prefer to be in touch with creation and typically morph into creatures such as Pegasi, unicorns, and even satyrs.

Able to mimic all life, they, like the Harrada and Draco, contribute to the culture of Heaven through their paintings and works of art. Gifted in tailoring and the beautification of one's physical form, their beauty is such that even Lucifer takes notice. When in their humanoid form, Issi possess wings similar to butterflies. Sariel was the former Prince, but sacrificed himself to expose the vulnerability of Abaddon. Azaziel now stands as Prince of his people.

The Issi also excels at all levels of herbalism and have now become healers as a result of the war. Issi can summon great celestial forces and target their enemies when in battle. Other angels from this house include Ashtaroth and Iblis.

Malakim: Sigil: Winged Feet

The angelic order of house Malakim are the messengers of God. If the Grigori are the eyes, the Malakim are its nerves. They constantly move to and fro throughout the realm, delivering messages from various groups and ministers to one another. Like the Grigori in their numbers, they are similar in that they keep Heaven's communication lines open.

The Malakim ride steeds called gryphons. Each angel has a steed that is actually obtained when they acquire their first assignment from their Prince. Only the Chief Prince, the Grigori, and the House are aware of the celestial home of the Gryphons. Able to move at incredible speeds, they are the fastest of all angelic kind. Gabriel, who is their leader, is the fastest and wisest. It is rumored that his speed rivals that of the Ophanim.

This has yet to be tested. All Malakim have wings on their feet and not on their shoulders as others of their kind. Malakim actually run, but their speed is so fast that they appear to fly. Malakim can also manipulate lightning.

Articles of War

When El exiled the Horde to the nether, He then placed within the Kilnstones of all angelic-kind His law that restricts the actions of our people. The following is understood by all Elohim concerning Elomic intervention in the affairs of men:

1. All souls are the Lords.
2. There shall be no interbreeding between species.
3. Humans shall not be brought into knowledge of your presence except through prayer or by voluntary submission to sin or by permission from El.
4. Agents of Lucifer may influence to their own ends human activity that humans have submitted themselves to, or through affairs of those who possess spiritual authority have yielded themselves to.
5. Members of the Host will not invoke the powers of the enemy, nor seek to derive and use powers apart from El's design. Doing so will constitute a rebellion, and those who do so will be marked as members of the Horde.
6. The ruling powers over a household, region or power will be held responsible for all those under their charge.
7. Any officer who shall presume to muster a human as a soldier (who is not a soldier) shall be deemed guilty of having

made a false muster and shall suffer accordingly.

The Shaun-tea'll will monitor the terms of these articles among both host and horde and shall have the power to imprison within Tartarus all who break them.

Thank You

Thank you for sharing in this fantasy series with me. More books are coming from me and I hope you will continue to follow my journeys. You can be notified of new releases, giveaways and pre-release specials at http://donovanmneal.com

If you loved the book and would like to be informed of other books, please make sure you sign up to my mailing list here. Feel free to leave a review!

Your help in spreading the word is gratefully appreciated and reviews make a huge difference in helping new readers find the series.

God bless you and I hope to see you within the pages of the next book!

Remember...there will be more stories so sign up for the mailing list!

About the Author

A lover of thought and the Bible, the Art of War and gaming. Donovan works professionally in the Human Services area and has a Master's degree in Nonprofit Management. He has over 20 years of service to the Christian community teaching the Bible as a member of the ordained clergy. Now retired from the clergy, Donovan has taken up his pen to express what has long been the untapped call God has placed in him to reach people through fiction.

Donovan's heart for ministry has carried into his secular pursuits and he has worked with countless abused and neglected children, adults with developmental disabilities, and women who have been victimized by domestic and sexual abuse. He has taught as an adjunct professor for several years and currently works full-time to secure employmentfor women who have had challegnes with housing. Donovan has three adult children: Candace, Christopher, and Alexander. He currently resides in Michigan with his wife Lynnette.

Made in the USA
Las Vegas, NV
11 September 2023